FJORD OF SILENT MEN

A paranoid Russian admiral . . . a CIA agent with a wife problem . . . a top military scientist with a sex problem . . . two ex-CIA men who turn freelance dirty-tricks operators . . . an undercover Mossad counter-terrorist squad with a life-or-death mission . . . plus a cultured KGB colonel and his mistress are just some of the ingredients in this swift-moving faction thriller . . . The plot turns on top-level, covert-action decisions taken in Washington, Moscow and Tel Aviv, resulting in international intrigue and mayhem.

PETER LANCASTER BROWN

◆

FJORD OF SILENT MEN

Complete and Unabridged

LINFORD
Leicester

First published in Great Britain in 1983 by
Robert Hale Limited
London

First Linford Edition
published 2004
by arrangement with
Robert Hale Limited
London

British Library CIP Data

Lancaster Brown, Peter, 1927 –
  Fjord of silent men.—Large print ed.—
Linford mystery library
  1. Detective and mystery stories
  2. Large type books
  I. Title
  823.9'14 [F]

  ISBN 1–84395–499–0

Published by
F. A. Thorpe (Publishing)
Anstey, Leicestershire

Set by Words & Graphics Ltd.
Anstey, Leicestershire
Printed and bound in Great Britain by
T. J. International Ltd., Padstow, Cornwall

This book is printed on acid-free paper

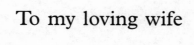

To my loving wife

The truth can be a better weapon than lies.

Home is the place where, when you have to go there, they have to take you in.

Robert Frost.

1

Admiral Nikolai Gronika, Commanding Officer of the Soviet underwater fleet, cherished one remaining ambition in his rapidly closing service career. It was born of years of frustration as a principal but passive role-player in a game called the Cold War. Had a team of psychiatrists had opportunity to examine the admiral, their unanimous verdict would have been that the subject had undoubtedly become an obsessive-neurotic — bordering on paranoia. For the world at large, such men in power or involved in leadership can be dangerous creatures and totally disastrous to the policies of a country. The Third Reich had perished because of one.

The admiral's problem was caused by the West's superior electronic know-how. Time and time again he and his commanders had been humiliated by the Americans and their NATO Allies. They knew every move his vessels made; if the Cold War ever became a Hot War, the Americans would know at the touch of a computer button precisely where to strike to immobilize every vessel of his entire fleet. At the Kremlin's Chiefs-of-Staff meetings he'd constantly lost face with the Politburo because so far he'd been unable to guarantee undisputed underwater naval supremacy if and when it was required. Before he retired, his dearest wish was to work a fast one on the Americans, and NATO, and then sit back to watch them squirm.

Had not other countrymen of his done it in the past with Sputnik, and then Yuri Gagarin's pioneer flight in space! For a time Hero Yuri Gagarin's face was the best-known face in the world. The Americans had been humiliated! He too, Nikolai Gronika, could be remembered in the glorious history of his country as another Hero who had inflicted humiliation on the Americans. And what was that old English expression . . . Ah, yes . . . The end justifies the means. He'd turn it round . . . The means would justify the end. *His means*: *his end*. A good joke, eh! A good Russian gallows' joke that would have the West shivering in their beds.

It would have to be done in absolute secrecy. Not even his Kremlin masters would know about it until he handed them the gift. He had just the man who could do it. He lifted his telephone to call his assistant in the office outside. 'Ah, Serge, tell Yankovsky I expect to see him tonight at my private reception.'

2

Academician Fyodor Yankovsky, Chief Scientific Officer of the Establishment of Military Defence (Navy Department) at Kazan, was extremely well thought of by his political and military superiors. He'd been a staunch member of the Komsomol in his teens at high school and a brilliant student. At Moscow University he'd graduated first in his class and joined the Communist Party as a full member. Now at the age of thirty-nine, and many honours later, his career as a Soviet high-flier was established. He already had all the privileges that Soviet élitism brought with it — a dacha in Grasnov just outside Moscow, seats for the Bolshoi at his command, and a carte blanche for foreign travel to all the international scientific congresses he wished to attend. By rights he should have been a happy and contented man.

For several months now he had been

working on a new, very top-secret project. Because of his past record, his masters tolerated his foibles and eccentricities, plus his often prima donna outbursts. After all, he was a world-class scientist — an egghead as well as a supreme practical technologist. He was a very rare bird indeed to nest in the glades of Soviet academia. Invariably the practical men were poor theoreticians; the theoreticians hopeless when trying to handle the practical aspects of new ideas. Dr Fyodor Yankovsky combined both abilities supremely. They were lucky to have such a scientific giant whose invention and application could match — perhaps, given the chance, outmatch — Western electronic military technology.

What the Soviet authorities did not know was that the chief scientist in charge of Admiral Gronika's personal top-secret 'Silent Men' project was a homosexual.

Yankovsky hadn't fully appreciated this himself until his university days were over. It was then he realized that his total lack of attraction to the opposite sex was not due *only* to the result of his preoccupation with his studies and the burning desire to succeed. As a student, while he'd laboured away with his books into the night, his classmates were often out womanizing. The thought of going to bed with one of his pretty female classmates can be said never to have entered his mind — let alone his loins.

He came face to face with his problem when he was holidaying in the sun at the Black Sea resort of Yalta just after he'd taken his PhD. He was twenty-three and had a brilliant career before him. It was the first time he'd ever relaxed in his life. The sight of those semi-naked female bodies he saw flaunting themselves on the beach actually repelled him. The thought of going to bed with one of them seemed horrific; yet his friends did it all the time. More disturbing to his thoughts was the realization that the sight of certain of the golden-haired male youths bathing with them caused him extreme pleasure.

He'd never consummated the sex act with another male until his twenty-ninth year when the International Society for the Study of Physical Science met in Paris and Yankovsky formed part of the Soviet delegation which attended there. Once, however, he'd tasted the forbidden fruits of male youth, there could be no going back to the life of total abstinence. Had not many of the great men of science and philosophy been homosexuals? Leonardo da Vinci, Humboldt . . . and scores of others he could name . . . Why should he not face facts? Yet, from now on he was very discreet in arranging his liaisons. If his masters ever discovered he was a practising homosexual, his career would be in ruins. Homosexuality was not tolerated at any level in public life within the Soviet Union. Homosexuals were only suffered, underground, to be used to compromise Westerners with aberrant tastes. They were tolerated in Soviet society like untouchables — as part of the distasteful KGB network for rooting out foreign spies.

Yankovsky restricted his sex life to his trips abroad. He made sure that he attended all the international scientific congresses open to him. He'd even been approached by the KGB to act as a part-time agent. Talking to Western scientists one might pick up all kinds of valuable bits of information. At once he'd agreed and believed he actually did feed back useful indiscretions he'd overheard in side discussions — particularly from American and British scientists who, he thought, were often very loose in the tongue about the military scientific projects they had advised upon. The KGB now sometimes suggested he attend obscure scientific conferences he'd not thought prudent he should apply directly to attend himself.

A few years back, when a colleague had been unmasked as a homosexual and suffered public ignominy and disgrace, Yankovsky had almost panicked and thought of defecting to the West. Round the research centre he knew he was often the butt of jokes about his bachelorhood. What if the powers that be should suspect him? There might be a witch-hunt! They couldn't prove any liaisons at home because there weren't any. What if the KGB secretly watched him when he was abroad? What if he was suspect already?

There was only one thing to do. Get married and allay suspicion! The thought of sharing a bed with a woman still repelled him. Yet it had to be done. He saw it now as his best disguise, but the prospect of the sex act with someone of the opposite gender was almost too horrible to contemplate.

With his logical scientific mind he thought round the problem for several weeks. He drew up a list of candidates. At the top of the list was Masha Levsky. She worked in the laboratories at Kazan. She ranked several steps down from him in the scientific hierarchy. At coffee-breaks he'd overheard his colleagues telling stories about her. There'd been snickers and grins when the story got round. She was still a spinster at twenty-seven. A pretty one. Reasons she hadn't got married, the story went, she was afraid of men. At the age of fourteen she'd been brutally gang-raped by students at her high school.

He went out of his way to be kind to her. He had her promoted as one of his personal assistants. She was highly flattered by his attention. He praised her work. On her part she recognized for the first time a man who might make a good husband. She saw them working together as a husband-and-wife team of latterday Curies. Ignoring his pale face and hangdog eyes, he was quite handsome in some ways. Soon he was her 'darling Fyodor'. Their whirlwind courtship was the talk of the research establishment. When he proposed, she accepted without hesitation. If anyone previously had entertained doubts about Yankovsky's brand of maleness, all such doubts were now allayed.

He'd picked his victim with consummate care. Their first night was a fiasco. After his first clumsy attempts she begged him with tears in her eyes not to touch her. Everything went the way he had planned it. He soothed her understandingly. He would give her all the time she needed to adjust to the physical intimacies of marriage. She should never mention it to him again. If, later, Masha Yankovsky was often puzzled and perplexed by her husband's infinite patience, she never once suspected his motives. The marriage otherwise had been excellent. Not all men were brutes; there were more ways to a happy marriage than those distasteful physical romps on the bed. She had been a very lucky girl indeed to have found such an understanding man.

It wasn't until the International Physical Society met in Hamburg, now some three months back, that the intelligence on both sides of the Iron Curtain had their first inklings of Yankovsky's some-time deviate behaviour.

3

Thirty minutes after leaving her base in Murmansk, a Soviet Kalinin-class nuclear-powered submarine, designated K3, was already a part of a highly computerized NATO surveillance package.

As soon as the first coded message had been transmitted to the joint NATO/US Navy Surveillance Group in Scotland — via the sea-bed passive sonar beacons (electronic 'Bloodhounds' Mark 5s) — she had been identified by her characteristic engine and hull noises as K3. She was an old acquaintance of the boffins in Scotland, and henceforth her hourly course progressions were monitored and stored on computer tape.

Rear-Admiral Noah Manners, US Navy Chief of the North West Europe Surveillance Group, was told about K3's progress and course adjustments on his routine morning's briefing held in the secret concrete bunker just south of

Aberdeen. For the first day, as K3 crept along the southern Barents Sea, she was listed as 'query' among routine 'Enemy' patrols. It was on her second day out from Murmansk, after she'd turned the corner and headed south along the Norwegian coast, off the usual track of Soviet submarine patrols, she was picked out for extra special surveillance.

Royal Air Force Nimrods operating out of Kinloss had picked her up soon after she'd rounded North Cape. From now on she would be watched constantly by passive sonars on the ocean floor, aircraft and military satellites — designed and launched for such purposes — until she returned to her base or she passed out of the jurisdiction of the North West Europe Group into some other group's domain.

Even if she dived under the ice of the North Pole or voyaged round the Antarctic circle, she would be followed relentlessly — her round-the-clock movements plotted to within a pinpoint accuracy of a few yards of her true position and the information stored on tape to be called up at a second's notice.

The combined NATO and US Global Surveillance Group prided themselves they'd never lost an 'enemy' ship yet. Of course, the Russians knew they were under constant watch, but they couldn't do a thing about it. Over the years they'd tried numerous dodges — laid many false trails — to try to disguise the 'fingerprints' of their under-sea fleet and confuse the West's deadly 'Bloodhounds'. By now they were almost resigned to the fact that although they had superior numbers at sea, they were no match for the West's electronic wizardry. Admiral Nikolai Gronika, however, now thought differently . . .

On day three of K3's voyage, when she was reported at the briefing as still heading south along the Norwegian coast, Rear-Admiral Manners turned to Commander Nick Sinclair, his chief exec: 'What do you think K3's up to this time, Nick?'

'Probably just another fjord recce, like she did last year. Remember, sir?'

The admiral remembered only too well. On that voyage K3 had been sighted off Balestrand, over 60 miles up the Sognefjord, by a Norwegian civilian who recognized what he'd seen. The damn fool Russian captain had chosen to surface just as a tourist car-ferry to Vik was moving ahead of her track. The Norwegian press had raised hell about Russian submarines invading Norwegian fjords and had asked the authorities what they intended to do about it.

They intended to do exactly nothing, but they couldn't tell the press that. If they'd told the press the truth that Russian nuclear-powered submarines, carrying intercontinental ballistic missiles, made regular sorties inside Norway's long, deep fjords, there might be widespread public panic. Yet among the West's military leaders, the presence of armed Soviet submarines inside the territorial waters of NATO powers raised no eyebrows these days. That they came to spy was accepted as one of the facets of the Cold War. And what were they going to do about it anyway? Blow up a Russian submarine with depth-charges! What about those deadly ICBMs and the

nuclear motors of the submarine itself?
The Swedes faced the same problem in
the Baltic from over-curious Soviet subs.
Attacking — provoking — the intruders
would only be asking for real trouble. The
Russians knew it too. No one in the West
was going to start a global holocaust just
because the Russians poached in their
neighbours' waters for a quick look-see at
NATO defences.

To a degree, NATO defence chiefs
welcomed the presence of Russian submarines. In that way the backroom boys
discovered quite a lot of technological
information about how Russian subs
operated. The boffins called it 'Field
Studies'. It was all grist for the mill in
case the real thing ever came about.
Anyway, NATO subs played similar
games inside Russian territorial waters. It
was tit for tat — quid pro quo — and, so
far at least, the military leaders on both
sides knew the ground-rules of the game.

On this last occasion when the Norwegian tourist had spotted the imprudent
manoeuvre of K3's captain, NATO public
relations had supplied a cover-story to

help out their Norwegian counterparts. The Russian submarine had actually been photographed diving again by the tourist. A nuclear-powered submarine, as such, could not be denied. Fortunately the picture was out of focus. It was leaked by Norway's Secret Service that the vessel in fact had been a United States' vessel on North Sea manoeuvres, miles off course. That was bad enough because Norway, officially, even though a member country, had consistently refused to have NATO atomic-powered weapons stationed on her soil. Others, of course, knew differently. The Soviets knew differently, but the official, non-nuclear-weapon stance was widely accepted as true by the Norwegian people. There'd been tongue-in-cheek promises to the press from Norway's NATO chiefs that Norway would dress down the US authorities in the strongest possible terms. It wouldn't happen again. The balm applied, the affair soon blew over.

On the morning of K3's sixth day out from Murmansk, Admiral Manners and his executive were a trifle perplexed when it appeared the Russian submarine had ignored and passed all the deep-water fjords on the west and south coasts of Norway and was now reported as stationed in 600 feet of water, lying off the port of Horten, halfway down the Oslofjord, about 40 miles south of Oslo.

'First time they've been to the Oslofjord visiting,' confirmed Commander Nick Sinclair. 'I hope her captain doesn't show his slip this time. There's a mighty lot of shipping toing and froing along that neck of water.' He turned to a man in naval uniform wearing two-and-a-half rings, who was sitting further along the briefing-table. 'Isn't that right, Per?'

'*Fa* . . . I mean, yes. That is correct,' said the Norwegian.

Admiral Manners looked round the table at his subordinates. 'Can anyone think of a reason why they've chosen the Oslofjord this time?'

Round the briefing-table — in addition to himself and Nick Sinclair — were Commander Terence Hawkins, Royal Navy; Group Captain Paddy Cavendish, Royal Air Force; and the newcomer

Kommandörkaptein Per Havik, a liaison officer from the Norske Marine, Bergen, who'd been specially flown over the previous night to advise on local problems if K3 was intent on poaching again inside Norwegian territorial waters.

The admiral's invitation was open for any officer to speak, but everyone knew it was really directed towards the Norwegian visitor. Everyone was now focused on Per Havik as he cleared his throat. 'I have prepared a slide with the assistance of Commander Sinclair. I think it will be a good idea to project it while I talk. With your permission, sir,' he said, conforming to pecking-order protocol and looking towards the admiral.

The admiral nodded acquiescence. He liked graphics at briefings. Something to hold on to — especially when foreigners were talking who were often hard to follow. However, he'd already noted that Per Havik's English was impeccable. He spoke the language better than most Americans he knew. He anticipated having no trouble following the Norwegian.

The room was darkened and the

operator, a chief technician USN, flicked on the slide-projector.

'I wish you to notice, gentlemen,' began Havik confidently, 'that the slide is a reproduction of part of the Oslofjord. To be precise, it is part of a chart: Den Norske Kyst, Oslofjorden, Number 3. It shows the relevant part of the fjord where K3 is reported to be stationed. Her position is . . . is here,' and using an arrow-image flashlight he indicated the exact location for his audience.

For the next ten minutes Havik went on to point out the salient geographical features round about . . . : The port of Horten; the industrial papermaking town of Moss on the opposite bank; Holmestrand; the old Viking seaport town of Tönsberg — where Havik happened to have been born. 'In Tönsberg,' he said, 'we have a saying that we were a town when Oslo was just an obscure village . . . ' He paused, but his parochial in-joke went unrewarded. He cleared his throat, nervously. 'Over here,' he pointed, 'is Hankö where our royal family go yachting.' Then switching across the fjord again, 'Here is the old Viking graveyard called Borrehaugene . . . ' Now he sensed the impatient shuffling in the direction of the admiral. Quickly, he moved on, 'And here, of course, is the fort of Bolaerne, the first defence line of the fjord,' and switching his arrow even more quickly to the extreme top of the projected image, 'Here we have Dröbak, the second line of defence in the Oslofjord . . . '

'Fine, fine. Lights, please,' cut in the admiral, a little weary of the travelogue. 'So you think the Russians have come to spy out those two forts you've just mentioned . . . Bolaerne and Dröbak?'

The name Dröbak had triggered the admiral's memory. His thoughts went back forty years. Naval history *was* his forte. 'Dröbak . . . the Dröbak Narrows, wasn't that where your boys sank the *Blücher* back in '40? The day the Germans invaded you?'

'That is correct, sir. The 14,000-ton German cruiser still lies there and she could be a hazard if a submarine dived over her position. However, the position of the *Blücher* is well known. Her hull is inspected regularly by naval divers. You see, she is now both a German war grave and a potential ecological hazard. Shall I explain?'

'Please go on,' replied the admiral.

'Most of the crew went down with her — hence her present role as a war grave. For that reason, and one other, my government have long resisted proposals by salvage companies to raise her. The other reason — the ecological reason — is that *Blücher* sank with her oil-bunkers full. It is feared that disturbing her would cause all the bunker-oil to spill out. If that happened in the Dröbak Narrows, it would pollute the whole of the fjord and bring disaster . . . '

'But surely,' interrupted the admiral, 'Those tanks forty years on must be highly corroded. That oil could spill out any time. You've got yourselves a real time-bomb there.'

'Not quite true, sir. Let us say, owing to excellent German workmanship and high-quality steel, the life of those bunkers is believed to be at least another fifty years. Perhaps more. The philosophy of my government is that salvage techniques in the future will have progressed to a stage where it will be easy and safe to tap off that oil. Meantime the situation is status quo.'

The admiral's thoughts were already a jump ahead. 'Any chances, you think, the Russians plan a dirty-tricks operation to bust open the *Blücher* to release that oil and cause embarrassment and hazard to a NATO member country?'

'No chance of that, sir. The area surrounding her is heavily mined. The Russians are sure to know it's mined. They wouldn't risk poking about anywhere near by.'

'Then what the hell *are* they after!' exclaimed the admiral impatiently. He'd expected a definitive answer from this morning's briefing — that's why he'd specially called in Norwegian expertise. 'Let's get back to the Bolaerne and Dröbak forts. How about those?'

Unruffled, the Norwegian replied: 'I doubt it, sir. As you know we used to have our main naval base in the Oslofjord at Horten; then we moved it to Bergen in the middle 1960s. There's absolutely nothing new for the Russians to be interested in at Bolaerne or Dröbak because both are obsolete — there's nothing to defend any more in the Oslofjord.'

'What about economic targets?' enquired the admiral.

'Only the Norske Esso oil refinery at Slagenstangen,' replied Havik. Since the room lights were now on, he rose from his chair and left the table. He walked over to the screen where the image of the chart was still projected. 'It's just here, a little to the south of K3's position,' he indicated, using his finger to point. 'It was built in 1960, just before Norway discovered her vast oil-fields in the North Sea. Geographically speaking it is now in the wrong position; emphasis has switched to the Stavanger region. Soon the refinery at Slagenstangen could become an economic white elephant. The Russians, of course, will know this, too.'

'Then we've drawn a blank, gentlemen,' announced the admiral with a throw-away gesture of his hands. 'What about you, Terence. Any comments?' Commander Terence Hawkins RN, from the traditional 'silent service', had none. 'And you, Paddy?' Group Captain Paddy Cavendish RAF was never one to indulge in unprofitable speculation.

The admiral sighed.

He turned to Commander Nick Sinclair. 'Okay, Nick, let's keep *extra*-special round-the-clock tabs on K3. Something about this one doesn't smell right. There's more afoot with Ivan this time than a simple look-see if *my* hunch is right. I think we should alert Naval Intelligence in the States and ask them to liaise with CIA on this one. Let's see what they can turn up. There could be something that someone hasn't told *us* about yet,' he added cynically.

K3 remained in the Oslofjord for another three days. For reasons unknown, she switched position at intervals of approximately 20 hours. At one stage, when she took up station not far away from where the *Blücher* had gone down and then proceeded to execute some odd manoeuvres, the admiral had wondered if his earlier theory had real substance. However 20 hours later she moved again — never having approached *Blücher* close enough to interfere in any way with the seabed wreck.

When the boffins reported that K3 was apparently on her way back to her home port of Murmansk and a few days later her echo blips disappeared off the passive sonars, after she docked, the admiral was still a puzzled man. It was no more than a hunch, but hunches in the past had earned him his very senior gold insignias and kept him at the helm while his Annapolis classmates were quietly retired to mufti.

In the weeks to come, US naval intelligence, at least, would have good cause to remember K3's odd manoeuvres in the Oslofjord. Meantime the cans of tape, accompanied by the buff-coloured operations dossier that provided narrative commentary to the electronic information, were filed away in the bunker's library.

4

Before leaving for the Hague, Academician Yankovsky *had* received a warning. The warning had been indirect but very definite.

He was no fool. He may have been one-track-minded yet he had the ability, like many scientists, to switch tracks at very short notice if it suited him. When, one evening, he came home from the military research establishment and saw that Masha had an odd gleam in her eye, he took note. When, after a specially delicious supper, she made unambiguous preliminary overtures that time was now ripe to share the secrets of their bodies and then hinted strongly that her long-suffering 'darling' Fyodor had been patient enough, he was immediately alert to the change in the status quo . . .

There had to be a reason for her change.

What had happened? Had someone been talking? Did the KGB or the GRU suspect he was a deviant? Did his wife suspect at long last she'd married a homosexual and she'd decided it was time to find out?

'What is it, my little *taiga* flower?' he enquired soothingly, meeting her embrace. He really was quite attached to her in his own peculiar way. She made the best borsch he had ever tasted. Even better than his mother had made! If he'd been potentially repelled by the prospects of any sexual union between them, he was by no means repelled by her obvious domestic talents. Like most men he really did appreciate those creature comforts a good wife provides. Marriage certainly had its rewards; but now they were treading on delicate ground, that potentially dangerous no-go area he'd managed to maintain between them. He really didn't want to re-enact that marriage-night bedroom scene and risk spoiling the genuine rapport that had grown between them since. Yet if she was making a play towards it, he'd have to pre-empt it quickly, *if* that's what she really had in mind.

But something was bothering her. He steeled himself to kiss her tenderly on the neck. 'Confess your secret to papa.'

'Promise you won't tell,' she replied coyly.

Jesus! women could be oblique, he thought.

'I promise.'

'Well, I've had visitors.'

'What kind of visitors?' He could feel the hair on the nape of his neck begin to rise.

'I promised not to tell, really. They said it could be psychologically inhibiting to women if their husbands knew about it.'

'Knew about what?' The mystery was deepening. Why couldn't she come out with it straight?

'If husbands knew that their wives were being asked highly personal questions about their husbands . . . Well, you know what I mean.'

'My love, I haven't the faintest idea,' he answered, trying to keep the shake out of his voice. God! What had she been up to?

Maybe it had not been a good idea after all that she'd left the research establishment after they were married to become a full-time housewife.

She looked away, unable to meet his eyes. 'About their personal love life together, silly.'

He felt himself break out in a cold sweat.

'What did you tell them?'

She hesitated and remained looking away from him. 'I said we make love at least three times a week. I lied. I didn't want to embarrass you, Fyodor. I have been a bad wife. Now I wish to become a good wife. Recently I have been reading magazines . . . '

He cut her short. 'Your visitors . . . Who were they? Where did they come from?' He felt utter relief, yet fear lingered in his gut.

'They said they were working under the jurisdiction of the Psychology Department at Moscow University. It's a new research group they've set up. They are researching into the sexual responses of the intelligent Soviet female. They were really very nice. They told me I was one of those specially picked out to help them. But Fyodor, I felt such a fraud! Such a cheat! . . . '

For a woman scientist she really was very simpleminded, he thought. She'd been taken in completely. Specially picked indeed! Of course she had been! Woman's vanity; it made her blind to the true purpose of their visit.

The KGB — or was it the GRU? — were experts at inventing new ploys to pry into the private lives of citizens. She was still babbling on in his arms, but he was no longer listening to her. He was busy thinking out ploys for himself.

He announced: 'Tonight, my little *taiga* flower, I must finish the paper I am writing for the conference in the Hague. We shall talk more about this when I come back from Holland. I have lots of patience.'

After he escaped into his study, he immediately helped himself to a generous vodka. He wasn't an habitual drinker. Too much alcohol clouded the brain and muddled one's thinking. It might be good for creative writers but not for creative scientists.

Tonight he had to think.

Those goons in the KGB or the GRU — or was it both? — suspected he was a homosexual. He'd seen through their trick straight away. Cunning bastards! Of course, in the West — particularly in America — that kind of investigation into peoples' sex lives was genuine enough. He'd read about the various Kinsey reports in foreign journals. But it didn't happen in the Soviet Union. The Russian people were different. It wasn't part of the Russian character to bare one's soul to outsiders — *especially* about sexual matters.

It had been a brilliant ploy by the KGB or the GRU and played with finesse to go unsuspected by Masha. He'd give them credit for that. When he thought about it more, perhaps if he hadn't had a guilty conscience, it might have fooled him too! What would those goons think of next in order to pry into the lives of honest Soviet citizens? There was no doubt, though, they knew *something*, and probably the net was closing in on him. His little Masha had unwittingly saved his skin to cover up her own deficiencies. If only she knew the truth of the matter! He felt a little ashamed of himself. Now she really did want to share the marriage bed.

His thinking came round full circle to thoughts which had preoccupied his mind for some time. Selfish thoughts which had no room for Masha. Defect to the West! In the West they tolerated homosexuality. Hadn't he read that in San Francisco there were thousands of homosexuals living fulfilled, open lives. His life in the Soviet Union was a sham. Masha would get over the shock. She'd divorce him and find a husband who could fulfil her needs too. He should get out while he could. Take something to the West that guaranteed he'd be welcomed and treated as a real VIP.

After he realized what must be done, he drank another vodka.

5

It had been Uri Cohen, the senior Mossad officer resident in the Oslo Embassy, who had been responsible for preparing the dossier on the activities of ex-CIA agent George Brand, alias Peter Hasler, plus other possible aliases yet uncovered. It was these field researches into the renegade American's participation in organized crime and his recent contact with known terrorists in Europe which was the reason Cohen had been flown back to Israel to brief his immediate chief Eli Weizmann.

Together they sat in Weizmann's office in Tel Aviv. The sign outside read: 'Israel Citrus Fruit Company'. No one in the neighbourhood, except the Israeli Secret Service, knew this was also the clearing-house for Mossad counter-terrorist activities in North-West Europe. It had a direct hot-line to the very secret Shin Beth headquarters just three blocks away.

The Mossad, since its uncertain beginnings in the early 1950s, had learnt to operate using the independent cell system within its own organization. Even senior operatives were kept in the dark about the activities of other departments and about personnel in the chain of command two steps below and two steps above them. Mossad agents never knew when their own people were watching them. The Shin Beth top brass lived in constant fear of KGB and GRU infiltrations. It had happened disastrously back in the early days with Israel Beer — a close confidant of the famous David Ben-Gurion himself. When the scandal broke, it was discovered that Beer was a Russian spy — a sleeper planted some twenty years before. It was believed that the organization was now clean, but you never knew.

Seated opposite his immediate chief, Uri Cohen drained his second glass of chilled orange juice. 'It's worth coming home just to drink some real kosher juice again. Where do you want me to start, Eli?'

'Naturally I've run my eyes over your

research dossier and, of course, that's why you're here. But you know me, Uri, I assimilate better straight from the horse's mouth.'

The two men had worked together for several years as senior career Mossad agents. Both had emigrated to Israel with their young families when in their early twenties. At home or socially they invariably spoke Hebrew, but in the office they usually drifted into the easy familiar New York vernacular of their upbringing. Both were graduate law students of Columbia; both were now fanatical Jewish nationalists who believed in the Homeland. Neither were orthodox, but neither drank nor smoked.

Uri Cohen straightened himself in the chair. 'I'll begin at the beginning. Let's take George Brand first — and we'll call him that because it's his real name. As we know, he turned rogue freelance twelve months back. In Norway and the rest of Europe he's known as Peter Hasler. He's got a forged US passport in that name as well as some other spare passports and aliases. As Peter Hasler he's got himself a respectable front as an importer/exporter . . . So far it's been mostly routine drug-smuggling. Not too much to worry us. However, what specially alerted me was that tip-off from one of my European stringers who told me that Hasler — I mean Brand — had been seen consorting in West Germany with known Baader-Meinhof riff-raff. We know some of those same people have strong fraternal connections with Black September . . . This then was something I thought could start to worry us — so locally we did our research project.

'What we've turned up is that Brand now also has some very unsavoury Norwegian connections: a cell of proto-Nazis containing some tough-guy ex-mercenaries among them. A few of their names are already known to us. I've gleaned a little background for one or two from our own files. There's a lot of stuff stacked away gathering dust when you start to dig . . . '

'There's too much goddam paper to read, Uri, that's the trouble with a desk job like mine. The paper just mounts up.

Look at it!' and he gestured with his open palms at the piles of paper on his desk top.

Cohen grinned back. Weizmann said, 'Mind if I jump ahead a little, Uri? Where does this Englishman fit in? One of Brand's dirty-tricks connections? Brand planning on opening a branch office in London? You say he puzzles you.'

'Right. A bit of an enigma this James Kerr. Could be a fellow traveller ... Could be a coincidence — *maybe*. You've read up on his background I presume? A freelance military correspondent with a roving commission in Europe for several British periodicals — plus that friendly connection with Olaf Solberg who in turn appears to be more than just a good friend of Brand's. Both Kerr and Solberg are ex-military tough-guys — British and Norwegian armies respectively. I gather they first met on some NATO exercise held in Norway ... Kerr resigned his commission for civvy street about two years back. Solberg about the same time. Funny coincidence that, but it could mean nothing at all ... '

'In your report,' cut in Weizmann, 'you mention that Solberg seems to help his sister in her import business. That could fit in nicely with Brand's respectable front. A nice causality?'

'I agree, except with Kerr it could be a mare's nest we've made for ourselves . . . '

'How come? Solberg is a 'business' friend of Brand's — you've proved that. Kerr's a friend of Solberg's . . . QED?'

'Sure, but Kerr's still the enigma. He sounds very bright . . . Before he joined the British Army as a regular, it seems he had the chance to go to Cambridge to read Natural Sciences. Instead he decided he wanted to play Action-Man . . . '

'Sure, I read that. So he's one of Nietzsche's mixed-up Dionysian/ Apollonian types and the extrovert side won out. Happens to a lot of us, Uri.'

'He's a lot interested in Norway . . . '

'I read that too. I also noted he's a crackshot and small-arms expert plus he's reputed to have this propensity for Wagner's music dramas . . . In my book that's quite a combo for a possible role as an employee of a macho-firm like Brand & Co . . . So I've missed your point somewhere?'

'Solberg's got a very attractive unmarried sister . . . '

'I saw that as well . . . And the thought hasn't escaped me either. Kerr could be sweet on her? It could be, as you're implying, an innocent hearts-and-flowers coincidence with no overtones . . . or it could just clinch it that all three are up to their necks.'

'Right. That's my assessment too. However, *I* can't forget either the medal Kerr won for gallantry fighting the IRA in Northern Ireland. The Brits don't publicize those awards for fear of reprisals on family and relatives. But unless Kerr's changed his spots, I can't see him rubbing shoulders with terrorist riff-raff like the Baader-Meinhof.'

'There's one way to find out . . . Could we recruit him?'

'I knew you'd get round to that one. Here comes my dénouement . . . '

Weizmann smiled and made a throw-away gesture with his hands. 'Don't ever

40

forget our past successes, Uri. We've planted some strange double agents in our time. This man, if he's clean, could be very useful to us.'

'Sure, but it helps their motivation a lot if they've got some Jewish blood or sympathy lurking in their family tree.'

'No Jewish blood? — no sympathy?'

'None at least the boys and girls in London could trace. They turned up something else though. Wait for it . . . It makes a good bottom line. They found out his uncle was a Brit Army sergeant killed by the Irgun outside Haifa in '47.'

'Okay, forget the double-agent bit, Uri.'

'I'd already figured it that way myself.'

'Let's now talk about our other 'friends' north of the border.'

'Okay, Eli, I've argued it this way: We know the Baader-Meinhof has a regular link-up with Black September. Now, what if Brand is thinking of expanding his dirty-tricks business and fancies himself as a terrorist entrepreneur? What if say Black September have in mind some more dirty tricks in Europe — say in this instance in a Scandinavian locale? Don't ask me what because at the moment I couldn't start to guess — but for argument's sake, let's suppose they have. Maybe Brand and his new strong-arm Norwegian connection could handle the subcontract for the whole job? Just think about it . . . In northern Europe you don't have too many dark skins about. They stick out like sore thumbs. Just say Black September for instance wanted to keep a low profile and they knew a subcontractor like Brand who'd be willing to take on a job at a price? When the balloon goes up, everybody could be looking for dark-skinned terrorists while some blond Vikings or rosy-cheeked Celtic types could be walking the streets incognito. Neat, don't you think? I hate to have to remind you, but remember that three-man Jap Red Army hit-team the Palestinians subcontracted to shoot up Lod Airport. That caught us with our pants down. I should hate that to happen again, someplace else . . . '

Weizmann, stroking his chin, said, 'I can think of something even neater, Uri. What if Brand himself thinks up a dirty-tricks op and sells the idea as an inclusive package deal?'

'You've a devious mind, Eli.'

'Don't say the same thought didn't cross yours too.'

'You bet it did, and I even thought about the people who might dig into their coffers to finance it . . . '

Neither man needed to name names.

Following the departure of Uri Cohen from the Israel Citrus Fruit Company Offices, to spend a well-earned and long-overdue week's leave with his family in the fashionable Tel Aviv suburb of Tazahala, Weizmann wrote up his own summary intelligence report to pass on to his immediate Mossad superior — the legendary Memuneh himself. Having finished this, he put his report, and the interview with Cohen, at the back of his mind and attacked some of the accumulated paper work mounting on his desk top.

The interview and his report limboed

in his mind a bare twenty-four hours. It surfaced again a split second after his grey matter comprehended the hot-line dispatch sent to him by Uri Cohen's stand-in at the embassy in Oslo.

6

The North Sea ferry to Kristiansand and Oslo sailed from the Hook on schedule at 1600 hrs. At the dockside office he'd picked up a cabin ticket hurriedly made out in the name of James Kerr and then followed the American aboard. He had shadowed Peter Hasler from his overnight hotel room in the Hague, and as far as he could tell, the target was unsuspecting and apparently travelling alone. He still didn't know why the American had travelled alone from Norway and was now returning there . . . One thing he did know: Hasler couldn't escape him before the ferry docked at Kristiansand at 1400 hrs the following day . . .

★   ★   ★

Two years before, Captain Kerr — now promoted major — had been discreetly seconded from the Ministry of Defence to work with the SOC — the Special Operation Commando, a top-secret NATO unit devised to combat international terrorism and all crimes associated with it. It was so covert that only the general who controlled its ops knew the various individual factions drawn together from Member Countries. At NATO Headquarters there were too many loose tongues and out-and-out spies to allow civil servants to pull any of the strings.

*   *   *

Now sipping coffee in the ferry's cafeteria, he reflected on what the general had said the day he'd briefed him and Olaf Solberg, his Norwegian undercover partner: *When you leave this room, you are on your own . . . You cannot expect any help if you get into difficulties. Absolute secrecy is our best safeguard . . . Once your cover as an agent is blown, you are no longer of use to the SOC. Whatever happens, we shall disown you . . .*

Except for those 'safe houses' scattered

about Europe and places they could pick up funds, they had no direct contact with their NATO ops room.

Now after the debacle in the Hague he was in trouble. Olaf was dead — murdered by Hasler . . .

He and Olaf had shadowed the ex-CIA man from Oslo through Denmark to Hamburg and then on to the Dutch capital. It was there the American had somehow spotted Olaf and then killed him. As part of their semi-independent undercover he and Olaf had always taken separate hotel rooms. He'd been due to relieve Olaf at 2 a.m. At midnight, Olaf, dying from a stab wound, had staggered into the bedroom. *It was Hasler!* . . . he'd said. Those were practically the only coherent words his partner had uttered before he'd slipped into unconsciousness and then died. Olaf had tried to tell him something else — about an embassy? but he'd never finished his story.

The immediate problem had been: did Hasler know Olaf had a partner? In coming to the hotel room, had Olaf blown both their covers? Had he come to warn him Hasler was on to him as well?

He recalled the general's briefing about Brand — now Hasler: . . . *This para-military operator is a gangster who deals in force, in terror, in violence. Your target is a breed apart . . . Even among his closest ex-colleagues this man is reviled with contempt . . .*

Olaf had finally managed to penetrate the Norwegian end of Brand's European narcotics operation . . . The general had been particularly interested in those neo-Nazis that Brand was involved with in Norway. Those people had been singled out for special attention. Their involvement had political overtones which had worried the general. It was the general, of course, who'd instigated the brief to keep a watchful eye on Hasler's activities in Europe — ever since the American had absented himself as George Brand from the CIA's Clandestine Services Directorate (known more euphemistically to Congress and journalists as the 'Department of Dirty Tricks'). Under the name of Hasler he'd set himself up as a freelance with Western Europe as his operations theatre. The general had believed that renegade ex-CIA dirty-tricks characters were dangerous people who were to be watched closely . . . Ambitious, highly motivated rogues might one day become involved in bigger things than narcotics.

He reflected that until the debacle in the Hague last night, he and Olaf had been one of the most successful undercover units in the whole of the SOC . . . They'd both operated under respectable civilian fronts. He as a freelance military correspondent; Olaf as part of his sister Anna's export/import business. Their cover jobs gave them infinite opportunity for European travel without raising curiosity from people who knew them. Before their respective secondments they'd met on a NATO exercise in Norway, and it was this long-term friendship that provided an additional part of their present covers in the event anyone should become over-curious why these two men should be seen together so often . . . He'd like to have been the one to inform Anna about her brother's murder, but this had not been possible.

. . . This time Hasler's trail had led to the Hague and now to the ferry. When Hasler had killed Olaf, it had triggered off additional complications. To maintain his own cover he'd had to abandon his hotel room without explanation to the staff. In doing so he'd automatically implicated himself. Bearing in mind the general's dictum: *Once your cover as an agent is blown, you are no longer of use to the SOC*, he'd got out quick to preserve his cover. Olaf was dead. The target had first claim. Lose him, and Olaf's death might be in vain. He'd picked up Hasler's trail at the hotel where Olaf had last been shadowing him . . .

. . . Nothing could be done now except in due course avenge Olaf's murder. Only by maintaining his cover would he succeed in that. The Dutch had put out an alert for the killer of Alf Backer — Olaf's undercover name. The man they wished to interview was a certain Philip Gill — the false name on the passport he himself carried in Europe this trip. At the Hook he'd bought his ticket for the

Norwegian ferry in his genuine name of James Kerr — sham Zapata moustache and all. No one, he hoped, would be looking for him under his own name, coupled with a facial disguise. His passports had been specially designed so he could substitute pages from one to the other at half a minute's notice. He'd frequently played the game of double bluff.

Once aboard the ferry he'd tracked Hasler to cabin 38. The American had booked a double cabin to himself. Now the ferry had sailed, Hasler couldn't go anywhere or meet anyone until they docked at Kristiansand . . .

After coming aboard, he had decided to eat all his meals in the cafeteria. He'd keep well clear of the waiter-service restaurant where he knew the American — fond of good eating — was bound to take his own meals. No point in showing his face too often — even his disguised face. The man's CIA record said he was highly intelligent *and* cunning . . . He and Olaf had underestimated the American's intelligence and cunning. Hasler would be alerted after rumbling Olaf. Now he'd be naturally suspicious of any slightly familiar face and draw obvious conclusions . . .

Still sipping his coffee and musing, he was vaguely conscious of someone moving towards him. Until the voice addressed him, he'd given the person scant attention. 'Mind if I share your table?' she said and jarred him out of his reverie.

Her accent was unmistakably Scandinavian-American. When she'd come out of partial eclipse, he could see she was a goodlooker. Quite a stunner in fact: great figure, tall, blonde, azure-blue eyes . . . all in all, very sexy. A cliché Hollywood-style Scandinavian.

He'd seen her before, somewhere?

She said cheekily, 'I thought from back there I recognized a familiar face.' She had a sly edge to her tone. She sat down opposite him, shot him a standard Colgate smile and removed a cup of coffee from her tray. 'But I still can't place you.' He felt his loins cool off and the hair on his neck bristle. She added, 'You a TV actor? . . . famous something?'

'Sorry . . . famous nothing,' he judged it best to answer in a civil tone. Why did this pushy bitch have to choose his table?

'Ah, well, a nice try,' she replied, giving her Colgate smile an encore. Then she began to sip her coffee. Between sips there were repeat toothy smiles, and about half a minute later she said, 'You think I'm a nosy parker?' Then added, 'Don't answer that . . . My name's Kara Alstad. If you were the other gender — and if you were Norwegian — it's a name that might ring a bell.'

'Sorry, no bells, Miss . . . Alstad.'

'Story of my life, Mr . . . ' and she flashed her teeth again while she waited for him to respond.

In truth a bell had tinkled. That's where he'd seen her face before . . . in one of Anna's magazines he'd browsed through a while back. But he wasn't going to let on. He didn't want to encourage her.

He saw her reach into her big shoulder-bag and then probe about. Finally she apparently found what she'd been searching for. She flicked out a card and pushed it across the table alongside his plate. 'I'm a journalist, see. I work with a magazine called *Norske Kvinner* — 'Norwegian Women' if you donta speaka da lingo.' She laughed brightly. 'You speak Norwegian, Mr . . . ?

'Smith . . . John Smith,' he replied without warmth. She'd realize he was brushing her off using a name like that. Perhaps now she'd drink up her coffee and push off. He'd better not encourage her. She sounded like a real female nosy parker. The kind that gave journalism a bad name. Pity though, he reflected. She was a genuine goodlooker. She'd provide a very sexy bit of cover to help while away the hours during the dull routine of a North Sea crossing. At any other time he'd have responded to that winning sexy smile of hers, but now his loins were positively cool. How the devil could he shake her off?

Before he could think up a suitable ploy, she'd begun to vamp him with one of those little-girl-lost routines that attractive female journalists use on male parties who are giving them a hard time with their copy. She tilted her head to one side and said, 'I still think I've seen you somewhere before ... What's *your* particular line M-r J-o-h-n S-m-i-t-h?' She enunciated the name deliberately slowly — disbelievingly — and held his eyes in her stare. Then she let her pink tongue slip out and run provocatively along her white teeth.

'Why don't you just drink up your coffee and then get lost, Miss Alstad.'

'Look, John,' she responded, affecting a wounded look as she played more theatre. 'I was born nosy, see. Don't hold it against me. When I walked into the cafeteria just now, you and your moustache looked the most interesting objects around ... Let's say you both qualify for a couple of reasons. And I'm always on the look-out for new, exclusive, copy. Our readers in Norway like stories about worldly, interesting people — especially worldly and interesting handsome male people with a few muscles in the right places.'

'I lead a pretty dull life, Miss Alstad. Your readers, I'm sure, wouldn't be interested in me.'

'Let me be the judge of that, John — and please, call me Kara. I've already called you John. More friendly, don't you think?'

She was like a terrier who'd caught a rat and just wouldn't let go. What the hell did she want of him?

A warning bell tinkled inside him. 'What did you say you wrote about in your magazine, Miss . . . sorry, Kara?' Might be best to humour her.

'People, like I said. I write a lot about people. A-day-in-the-life-of . . . that kind of thing. Famous people, ordinary people, creative people, interesting people . . . and especially people who've got problems . . . they're all grist for my mill. I often go out of my way to pick up hot, very exclusive copy . . . Okay, so I'm pushy.'

'Like now for instance,' he chipped in quickly.

She didn't answer him directly. She affected an enigmatic smile and went back to rummage briefly in her shoulder-bag. What she fished out he instantly recognized as a clipping from a Dutch newspaper. Watching his eyes, she pushed it across the table towards him. She exclaimed, 'Touché!'

He gave the clipping only a perfunctory glance and kept his eyes levelled. 'I don't understand what you're getting at, Miss Alstad?'

She looked momentarily uncertain and narrowed her eyes. 'I can be discreet,' she said.

'About what?' he answered flatly. 'Forgive me, I don't know what the hell you're talking about.'

She picked up the clip again and thrust it under his face. 'So you're not the man the Dutch Police are looking for?'

'I beg your pardon,' he said blandly. His mother had once told him he ought to take up acting professionally . . . but then, in a way, he had, hadn't he? Not quite the same as a stage career but still one requiring the use of his natural thespian talents. Then he started to laugh at Kara Alstad. 'Oh, now I see what you're getting at. *You* think I'm . . . ' and he picked up the clip to scan it. 'You think I'm . . . Philip Gill?'

'Aren't you?' she snapped back at him, her eyes narrowing again. 'Or is your real name James Kerr?'

My God! he thought inwardly. *Who the hell is she!* However, he kept his cool. At their training-school in Brussels they'd rehearsed surprise interrogation techniques as part of their SOC training. They'd been coupled up to lie-detectors so the instructors could judge the ability of their trainees to lie at time of stress. He'd graduated as one of their star pupils.

'I really must protest, Kara,' he said smiling. He'd call her Kara now. He wanted to find out how she knew his real name. She could have seen it on the passenger list, of course — *as a name* — but how did she know it was *his* name? 'I've told you my name is Smith, John Smith. Now you have to believe me . . . honest.'

'I don't believe you, John. Remember, I write a lot about people. I'm practically a female Sigmund Freud. Let's say I've picked up a few insights about human nature et cetera. Okay, I'm going to put you to the test. And I kid you not. After I spotted you sitting here, I dashed down to the Purser's Office. I wrote a short note to a friend I have on board. If I don't collect before 9 a.m. tomorrow morning, the sealed note will be opened and people will know who you *were* back in Holland . . . A bit dramatic, I know . . . but then I hadn't talked to you yet. I've a hunch we could help each other. I think people may have been reading you and Solberg wrong . . . ' She watched his eyes again as she enunciated his Norwegian partner's name. 'Now I know you're the cuddly-bear type on the side of law and order, I might get round to collecting my note tonight if you co-operate.'

'I've no idea what you're talking about, Miss Alstad . . . really I haven't.' He turned on the charm now. 'How can I co-operate to reassure you?'

'I want to know why you're following Peter Hasler. That's the major part of the story line I'm interested in . . . I'm a journalist interested in why you and your chum Solberg were following Hasler through Europe. I've followed you all from Oslo, so don't deny it. In case I'm not making myself clear, I'm offering my services as a Dr Watson. You'll need another working partner now you've lost Solberg. You'll also find I'm good at playing Girl Friday. My rewards . . . a share of the story when we've cracked it. I'm not forgetting either that together we could have a little fun on the way. I suppose you ought to know I have a healthy appetite for vigorous males.'

'Miss Alstad, I still don't know what the hell you're talking about.'

'We'll soon find out then, won't we — come nine o'clock tomorrow morning. That message to my friend is by way of a little life insurance — just in case you decided to . . . dispose of me.'

'Honestly,' objected Kerr, trying to keep his smiles going. 'I've never heard such a tale in my life . . . You're crazy.'

'Oh yeh? Well, we'll see then, won't we. Give me five minutes to freshen up and then come to cabin 64, boat-deck . . . We have things to talk about. But just remember, James Kerr, you've really got no choice, have you? I'm calling your bluff.'

★ ★ ★

Inside cabin 38 the man known aboard as Peter Hasler felt stifled and jumpy. He decided what he needed was a turn or two round the decks. Since last night he'd smoked too many cigarettes. Now what he needed was some bracing air to ventilate his lungs. He could perhaps use a coffee too . . . On the way he'd try the cafeteria.

He was in line at the check-out when he saw her again. No doubt at all the woman sitting at the far end was the same nosy-parker Norwegian journalist — Kara Alstad. Just a couple of weeks before she'd again tried interviewing him for one of her profiles. 'Americans in Exile' she'd told him was the name of the series she was running for that magazine in Norway which employed her. He'd given her the brush-off twice now.

Too much of a coincidence *this* time. Was she shadowing him? Was she in some way connected with that other Norwegian he'd got rid of last night? He'd believed that Norwegian represented authority of some kind . . . He wasn't sure now. He'd never found out because the man had got clean away before dying of that stab wound. The worries about that man had niggled away and continued to do so after he'd heard on the local radio the Dutch Police were looking for a Philip Gill who'd occupied the hotel room where Alf Backer's corpse had been found . . . Only Backer wasn't his name, it was Solberg . . . Olaf Solberg. From the very start there'd been something funny about this guy he'd taken on. That's why when he spotted him in Hamburg and then the Hague he'd got rid of him. In the high stakes he was playing for now he couldn't afford to take any kind of chance — not with someone like Backer who was expendable. Those boys of his in Norway were already checking on Solberg's sister. He'd phoned them first thing this morning . . .

Now, who the hell was this new character that Kara Alstad was chatting up? One of her profile victims? She was talking to him very confidentially. Something smelt wrong about this woman; his sixth sense told him so. The thought gestating a moment ago started to make sense. Could she be one of the Black September people? Anything was possible. Could it be they didn't trust him? Could it be the guy she was talking to was also a Black September man? You couldn't trust anything or anybody in this world. That's why he'd told no one what he was up to visiting Hamburg and the Hague again. Yes, the Black September could have put a tail on him. What better tail than a Norwegian blonde journalist! They wouldn't send a dark face after him because they were smart enough to know he'd rumble it.

He had to find out.

★   ★   ★

When Kara Alstad left the cafeteria, Kerr pushed his plate away and drained his coffee. He'd lost his appetite for food. If this bitch really wanted to turn him in, she could have gone to the Purser's Office and tipped them the wink who he was. The ship's Master-at-Arms and a few strong-arm members of the crew would see to the rest. Or did she like playing with fire? Was it that before she tipped off the authorities she wanted some hot copy in order to write an exclusive 'A-day-in-the-life-of someone on the run'? That would titillate her readers' palates right enough. She'd probably get a world-wide syndication on an 'As-told-to-Kara Alstad' scoop like that. But where did Hasler come in? How did she know about Olaf and the American?

Thinking back, he wondered how convincing he'd been in his denials. Trouble was she knew too much. Give her a chance and his cover would be blown. He recalled her parting words . . . She was right, she had called his bluff. Now he'd call hers.

Before he went to her cabin, he ducked into his own to brush his teeth. It was force of habit cleaning his teeth after he'd eaten, or drunk coffee. He was inside only a minute or two. Outside, as he closed his cabin door, he had a mild shock when Peter Hasler came walking by. He tried to keep his face straight and meet the American's stare coolly; then he strolled off looking for number 64. He didn't look back to see if Hasler was watching him.

He rapped three times on the door of her cabin before he walked in. He slipped the catch behind him.

There was no obvious trap awaiting him. Not unless, of course, he considered Kara Alstad was some kind of man-trap.

'Then you decided to come?' she said.

'Let's say you made the male in me curious. Your pick-up technique is a bit dramatic but original, I'll say that.'

During the five minutes' grace she'd performed a quick-change act. All part of her own theatrical repertoire? She was dolled up in a fetching pastel-green oriental-style chansong whose side-slit showed an indecent length of smooth white thigh.

At the sight of her, he felt his manhood rise. It had crossed his mind that alone with Kara Alstad there might be . . . *possibilities*, but the dress and the carnal, exposed thigh had taken him by surprise.

He stood there watching her.

In silence she poured him a large whisky. He waved away her gesture of water.

'Where do we go from here?' he said huskily and then knocked back his drink in one gulp.

'Business or pleasure first?' she purred softly, her face suffusing with a sly grin. Then she recapitulated her earlier trick of running her pink tongue provocatively over her teeth.

'Is there a choice?' he said.

'*I* like combining both.'

He moved towards her. Hesitantly he began to unzip her dress. Her mouth was moist, her lips parted and their tongues met. Reaching down, he began to stroke her exposed thigh softly. Then his hand went back to the zip and in one dextrous movement he disrobed her completely.

As he'd suspected, there wasn't a stitch of clothing beneath her dress. She nuzzled closer, her shapely, naked body moulding against his. He eased her away gently and then lifted her to the already turned-down bed. After he laid her head on the pillow, he quickly began to undress himself . . .

It was when he'd finished undressing and was preparing to mount her she caught sight of what to more casual eyes might pass off as a small, faint, odd-looking bruise high up on the inside of his right leg at a position normally disguised by the hang of the scrotum. He suddenly caught her stare.

'I like my men well set up,' she murmered reassuringly in his ear. Then, with thighs raised and spread, heels pressed into the small of his back, she met his first vigorous thrust, eagerly.

In their respective calls of duty, they made love with an intensity and urgency that quite surprised them both.

★   ★   ★

Two minutes after Kara Alstad had spotted the man who might be Philip Gill — alias James Kerr — she had made a ship-to-shore radio phone call to her control number in Oslo. When the party answered, she said, 'Felix, it's Hannah . . . Listen, I haven't much time. I think I've just spotted Solberg's friend Kerr — that's if it's not a look-alike. The point is I'm not absolutely sure I have the right man. That's why I'm phoning you, see . . . You've seen Kerr's detailed file passed on from London, I haven't. There must be something? Some feature that could clinch it for me . . . ?'

The man listening at the Oslo end scratched his chin. He revisualized the contents of the file he'd perused a week ago. He answered, 'Physically — only the results of an aberration he and some of his brother officers incurred after too many drinks one night . . . A very small blue tattoo inscribed inside his right-hand crotch. It reads Aff . . . stands for *Audaci favet fortuna*, 'Fortune favours the bold'. It's the regimental motto of his old unit in the British Army. You'll need X-ray eyes for that one — or a touch of *chutzpah* yourself, Hannah, to get the guy to drop his pants.'

Felix was still chuckling to himself as he put the phone down.

7

When it became clear in Moscow that Academician Fyodor Yankovsky had walked out of the Hague Conference and had apparently defected, there were those in high places who wanted to know *why* someone recently suspected of being a sodomite and engaged in top-secret military work had been allowed out of the country in the first place.

On receiving the news, Admiral Gronika suffered a heart attack and for the next few hours was in no position to offer any immediate answers. The full extent of the possible damage to Soviet foreign policy and nuclear strategy was not realized until shortly after 6 p.m. the following day . . .

★　★　★

Admiral Nickolai Gronika had learnt of Fyodor Yankovsky's *alleged* aberrant sexual encounter in Hamburg only a week before his chief scientist in charge of the 'Silent Men' project was scheduled to depart for the Hague to attend the forthcoming scientific congress to be held there. He learnt about it from the GRU who in turn had been put in the picture by the KGB. That it had taken several weeks to filter down to his level angered him. What's more, he didn't believe it either.

He was reassured that the GRU also concluded it was malicious foreign gossip purposely directed to one of the Soviet's foremost scientists and technologists. For once they'd also agreed with the KGB's findings.

For several weeks before informing their colleagues in the GRU, the KGB had checked into the background of Fyodor Yankovsky. They found his record of behaviour impeccable. There was not a shred of evidence of aberrant sexual behaviour *inside* the Soviet Union. The man was happily married. It had been confirmed by his wife. He was apparently a tour de force in bed! No, the whole thing *was* malicious gossip — put out by some Western intelligence agency because someone had suspected him of acting as a part-time KGB agent during his trips abroad to scientific congresses. Of course, he'd been their agent, and sometimes the information he brought back was considered useful. There could be no possibility he was a double agent. All the evidence pointed to a mischievous, unsubtle attempt to damn — by innuendo — the integrity of one of Russia's outstanding scientists. It was a Western ploy that had been exposed. Revenge by someone for past dirty tricks played by the KGB on prominent Westerners they'd actually caught and filmed in the homosexual act. If there had been a photograph of Yankovsky performing the act, that would have been a different story. There was no film; simply innuendo with no supporting evidence.

They'd tried, of course, (as Western intelligence networks had tried) to recheck the source via the freelance stringer who'd given the story to the KGB agent responsible for the feed-back.

That the stringer, after feeding the poison, had now gone to ground was highly suspicious to the KGB as it also was to the consensus of Western intelligence.

When Yankovsky's application to travel abroad went before the 'Excursions Committee', chaired by the admiral himself, it was duly authorized. The admiral considered there was no risk. Yankovsky, after all, had served him well. After listening to the admiral's personal specification for a secret weapon, he'd devised and tailored the 'Silent Men' project to fit the bill. And everything *had* been kept secret. Even the GRU and the KGB apparently didn't know what was going on. Such was the measure of their success! He'd need Yankovsky's good-will and advice again when he took the wraps off the project and explained his new, deadly Cold-War bargaining weapon to the Kremlin bosses.

His 'second-strike' Silent Men missiles were immune to retaliatory knock-out in time of crises or actual war. Unlike his underwater fleet which could be destroyed by the Americans at the touch of a computer button, the Silent Men missiles now in place were truly inviolate! If it came to a real confrontation, the West, duly informed of their presence in the Oslofjord, would realize they couldn't retaliate. If they did, they would be putting at risk the Norwegian peoples — their NATO Allies! The fact that the missiles were now in position and subtly booby-trapped with sophisticated electronic devices prevented the Americans, or anybody else, from trying to disarm them. Without full knowledge of the sequence of the electronic codings — and the only copies of them were in the admiral's own safe — no one could disarm or even approach them. A wrong signal or no signal and the whole lot would go up in smoke!

The Silent Men missiles were bargaining weapons which, when the time came, would have untold possibilities.

He'd timed and stage-managed the announcement for the forthcoming meeting in Moscow of the Joint Chiefs of Staff. At that particular venue it would have maximum impact on the representative audience of the Politburo. It would automatically spoke the arguments of any of those upstarts who wished to usurp him as Commander-in-Chief of the Soviet undersea fleet. Admiral Nikolai Gronika and his chief scientific officer would be the talk of Moscow!

★　★　★

The Soviet president had just begun his evening session with the Politburo when the unexpected call from Tel Aviv came through. Meantime, events elsewhere had been running their course.

The text of the threat which had been delivered anonymously by hand to the Israeli Embassy in Oslo purported to come from an organization which called itself the 'Friends for Peace.'

At first reading, the ambassador himself believed the crude threat, written in Hebrew, was just another hoax. This was his natural reaction. Although prima facie it was the most terrible threat he'd ever chanced to read, hoaxes of one kind or another had been a constant source of irritation to Israeli embassies and consulates since the new State had been founded. However, while it was now appreciated that the vast majority of threats were mischievously conceived, all were, nevertheless, checked out. This was the job of the resident Mossad officer.

At first glance the stand-in Mossad officer shared the ambassador's opinion. It was probably a spoof. Yet this one was dressed up to cast doubt and then fear even among the most cynical and blasé of Israel's foreign-service personnel. Never in either's experience had a threat been more ominous. Threats to assassinate, bomb, murder or rape Jewish employees — yes. They were routine by now, but this threat was so fantastic perhaps it had to be taken seriously. Over the years the Mossad officer had developed an instinct that enabled him to distinguish between the spoofs and the genuine threats. When he reread the message for a second time and then paused to reflect, a frisson suddenly ran down his back.

★ ★ ★

In Tel Aviv the prime minister was now convened in emergency session with the top brass of the Shin Beth. Was it hoax, bluff or verity? Would Israel be bombarded by Soviet-built Silent Men missiles located in Norwegian territorial waters if she did not comply with the conditions of the ultimatum received a few hours back at her Oslo Embassy? An ultimatum and threat that demanded Israel must close down and then proceed to dismantle her top-secret nuclear research station at Dimona near Beer-sheba. A time-limit ultimatum of ten days had been stipulated. If by then the Israelis had not complied, missiles with nuclear war-heads would be directed at Dimona itself.

The faction in the Shin Beth comprising the military intelligence — the Agab Modi'in — were inclined to dismiss it as a hoax or at best a brazen bluff made by some new Palestinian organization. The chief officer of the civilian Mossad — the Memuneh, its titular head — also had initial reservations. However, he'd just read the secret report about George Brand sent him by Eli Weizmann. Were Weizmann's worst fears being realized? There must be doubt. Doubt because there was a plausible alternative hoax-cum-bluff theory that both the Agab Modi'in and he subscribed to as a strong possibility. It could be some cunning Soviet-inspired trick — orchestrated via the KGB — to get Dimona closed down. A trick using this organization calling itself 'Friends for Peace' as a front. Trouble was the Mossad had also received news that top Russian scientist Yankovsky might have defected, but no one knew if this was just a rumour. The Americans, it seemed, didn't admit to holding him. For the moment all the news would be kept from the Knesset. Even if the threat were a hoax or bluff, it was the kind of thing to get the Israeli Parliament into a panic. This could be exactly what the Palestinians — or/and the KGB? — had intended should happen. First things first: the Israeli prime minister would talk with the Soviet president, privately, to see how much real substance the threat carried.

While the prime minister talked to the Soviet president, the Memuneh was already on another line contacting Eli Weizmann . . .

* * *

In the Kremlin the Soviet president was visibly annoyed when the chamber usher approached and then interrupted him with the whispered news from his private secretary that the prime minister of Israel was calling him direct from Tel Aviv.

Would the usher pass back a message to his private secretary to tell the Israeli prime minister he'd phone him back in about one hour's time when the Politburo's urgent business was over. Really, this interruption to the Politburo's emergency session was too much; there was enough on his mind with the consequences resulting from the defection of Academician Yankovsky without having to face the possible wrath of the

Israeli prime minister over some new trivial anti-Zionist act the Soviet Union had now supposedly committed. This was the trouble with having a fluent Russian-speaking Israeli prime minister. The man was forever ringing direct to Moscow. Personal hot-lines between capital cities were sometimes too much of a good thing.

Before the Soviet president could pick up the threads of his discussion with his ministers again, there was a fresh interruption. This time it was the private secretary himself who appeared. 'I beg your pardon, comrade President. The Israeli prime minister insists he speaks with you, *now*. He says the subject-matter is most urgent.'

'Very well, if he must.' After making apologies to his ministers and then whispering a few words in the ear of his deputy, he retired to the anteroom to use the phone-connection there. 'What's on your mind this time, Isador? . . . '

Five minutes later a very gloomy Soviet leader returned to the chamber and announced: 'Alas, comrades . . . we have further troubles . . . '

In Tel Aviv the prime minister's own news relayed back to the senior officials of the Shin Beth was, on the face of it, more reassuring if not exactly truthful. ' . . . He's readily admitted that Yankovsky is missing,' he announced. 'They presume he's defected to the Americans. He suggests we'd better check with Washington . . . However, he's denied as totally preposterous any idea that the Soviet Union had allowed some of its tactical nuclear weaponry to fall into the hands of terrorists. He believes it is a mischievous hoax made in very bad taste . . . He suggests the CIA's behind it.'

'But do we believe him?' said a top official, voicing his doubt.

'Until we know better ourselves,' answered the prime minister, 'we almost have no choice.'

Twenty minutes later the Memuneh was secretly briefing Weizmann in the upstairs office of the Israel Citrus Fruit Company.

In Moscow the new horrors were being faced. Six hours after the Israeli prime minister had rung off, the inner circle of the Politburo knew the full extent of the happenings. (a) Admiral Gronika, unilaterally and in secret, had seen fit to implement his own Cold-War strategy and put at risk the fragile détente with the West. (It was now apparent the admiral *was* mentally disturbed and, notwithstanding his weak condition, he was immediately transferred to the Moscow Psychiatric Institute.) (b) — And this was perhaps the worst part of the horrors — the Americans had likely been offered on a plate the latest secrets of Soviet nuclear weaponry and at the moment they might even be in the very act of plucking working examples of it from the seabed somewhere inside Norwegian territorial waters.

Heads were now rolling in the USSR . . . Admiral Gronika's had been the first. Another directly in line for the chop was that of Colonel Stephan Zigel — a past star performer in the echelons of Lubyanka. That his head so far had remained in place was due partly to his past record and mostly to his very efficient interrogation of the admiral himself, following receipt of the gloomy news passed on from Tel Aviv.

Without resort to drugs or torture, the colonel had skilfully extracted the full extent of the dying admiral's paranoiac aberrations. Calls made by the colonel to Yankovsky's scientific associates and co-workers had also confirmed the worst.

Understandably the colonel had no wish for his own head to roll. Fortunately he had a strong survival instinct. You did not become a star KGB performer within the portals of Lubyanka without also becoming an expert in the cut and thrust of KGB politics. Two of Colonel Zigel's other qualities were a sharp analytical brain and a cool head in a time of crisis.

As the crisis hours ticked by, it was the colonel who became less certain that Yankovsky was already in the hands of the Americans. The KGB's international listening network, especially alerted to the name of the Soviet Academician, had so far drawn a blank. The KGB's double agents, infiltrated into the intelligence departments of every Western nation, had likewise so far reported no sign or indication of Yankovsky's whereabouts. However, what they were reporting back to the colonel was a universal and curious professional interest in what organization it could be who'd actually acquired Yankovsky's services. The Americans seemed specially curious. Of course, this could all be part of some game of double bluff. Didn't the Soviets themselves indulge in games of double — even triple — disinformation bluffs. Someone out there could be keeping very quiet about Yankovsky defecting to them. Whoever it was would immediately realize that the Russian Academician was potentially the most valuable prize ever to walk out of the Soviet Union.

The Americans, however, were the ones he knew they should really concentrate on. The Americans had a very precise and set format for dealing with escapees from the USSR and the Eastern Bloc. They were *all* handled by the CIA's defector reception centre at Camp King near Frankfurt, West Germany. It was there,

Colonel Zigel knew, all grades of defectors were subjected to intensive debriefing and interrogation by the agency's experts. He'd heard that questioning sometimes lasted months; he'd known cases — when the CIA suspected KGB infiltrators — where defectors were interrogated for a year or more before they were allowed to travel on to the United States.

It was most significant, then, that the colonel's inside man at Camp King was very positive that Yankovsky wasn't being held there. However, a problem still confusing the Soviet's military experts was separating fact from speculation. Colonel Zigel's interrogation of the admiral, and later his and others' more detailed interrogation of Yankovsky's assistants and co-workers, gave cause to assume that the four Silent Men missiles dropped in their sub-surface launching pods by the Kalinin-class submarine were actually booby-trapped with sophisticated electronic devices — remarkable devilish inventions of no other than Yankovsky himself. The real horror to be faced was the likelihood that only Yankovsky knew the correct coding and decoding combinations for all these devices. Codes and decodes were supposedly held in the admiral's secret safe, but it was more than a probability that Yankovsky had substituted false ones just before his defection. Indeed — horror of horrors — the records in the admiral's office showed that Yankovsky had had access to the safe only a few days before leaving for the Hague Conference.

Interrogation of the experts had revealed that the missiles were designed to be activated/deactivated targeted/retargeted at a stand-off remote-control distance of up to 5 kilometres. All these adjustments could be made with a battery-operated micro-chip contrivance only a little more complicated than that used to control model aircraft or boats. It was yet another brilliant innovation of Yankovsky's practical technological genius. Another alarming factor was the realization that Yankovsky could pass on the operative know-how to any normally intelligent lay person. Once Yankovsky had shown them how, the Academician himself was dispensable.

It had soon become clear too that if someone — even an equally knowledge-able expert — tried to interfere without knowing the correct codings and decodings, the booby-trap devices would immediately trigger the nuclear war-heads. If the Soviets themselves tried to disarm and remove the missiles without being sure of the procedures — and nobody so far was sure they were! — it would herald a Scandinavian nuclear holocaust.

The conflict facing the Soviet president was whether he should make a clean breast of things and tell the Norwegians *in secret* what had happened. Tell them, whatever else they did, not to allow the Americans into their territorial waters to interfere in any way with those missiles. But the Norwegian government would likely throw a very *public* fit if the Soviets told them the truth. If the Norwegians or their Scandinavian neigh-bours discovered that lying in the deeps of the Oslofjord were sundry megatons of nuclear explosives which were *possibly* in control of unknown terrorists, public law and order might be put at risk. The panic, knock-on, domino effect might even spread as far as the Soviet Union! No, after due deliberation, the Soviet president decided he couldn't bring himself to tell the Norwegians the bad news, yet. Then, alternatively, what about engineering a leak to the CIA about the Silent Men missiles. A disinformation leak with the added message that Yankovsky was a madman bent on world destruction and who had been about to be incarcerated in a psychiatric institute but had cunningly fled the USSR to avoid it. They could create a double doubt in the Americans' minds — a serious doubt about the safety of the missiles *and* one about the defector's sanity. The CIA's influential Forty Committee that curbed the extra-curricular activities of the American Secret Service would procrastinate at length before giving permission for a covert operation to pick up any highly lethal Soviet booby-trapped missiles in the Oslofjord ... The Soviets could almost bank on that. Meantime, if Yankovsky wasn't already in American hands, he *might* be found. This was a field operation for the KGB.

8

Jake Kovas had just got out of bed in his rented downtown Washington condominium when the phone jangled and the long-distance operator told him there was an overseas person-to-person call for him. 'This is George . . . ' the familiar voice began — and from that moment the adrenalin began to pump . . . By the end of the veiled transatlantic conversation it was pumping prestissimo when George said, ' . . . So we meet to discuss, eh? . . . I'll wire your KLM ticket, pronto.'

After he replaced the phone in its cradle, he knew that this was the big one. The one he'd been waiting for . . . George wouldn't have asked him in otherwise. He recognized his own days with the Company were now numbered.

★ ★ ★

To be caught flagrante is an emotive experience; the expression itself conjures up the horror of the occasion. The disturbance caused by the sudden blast of light from the beam of a flashbulb, while engaged in the unnatural sexual act with a teenage Dutch boy in one of the Hague's most notorious public brothels, had the expected traumatic effect on the composure of Fyodor Yankovsky.

The trap had been laid and sprung. It worked like a charm. The man who'd masterminded it was ex-CIA agent George Brand, alias Peter Hasler. The planning, the inquisition and the browbeating afterwards were assisted by his new partner Jake Kovas.

All had been made possible because of the snippet of information routed from one of Brand's ex-freelance stringers in Hamburg, a contact from his CIA days. It is the chain reaction resulting from such snippets of gossip that has been known to determine the course of nations.

When the 26th International Congress for the History of Physics was held three months previous at Hamburg University, word had been dropped from a certain male homosexual prostitute that one of his clients had been a Russian. The stringer overhearing the remark — he was paid generously by his own clientele to be alert for such interesting gossip — followed it up with a little find-the-joker research.

There could be no doubt that the man concerned was the top Soviet scientist Fyodor Yankovsky.

The stringer immediately thought of George Brand who as far as he knew was still an agent working with the CIA dirty-tricks (Clandestine Services) Directorate. Brand could definitely be very interested in this one and he had a reputation for paying high prices. However, the livelihood of a freelance stringer is a precarious one — the real coups were few and far between. One had to take full advantage of information received and make hay while the sun shone. He dropped the same story to his contacts with the British SIS; the French SDECE; the West German BND (the local equivalent of the CIA); the BKA (the local equivalent of the FBI); the Mossad; their colleagues and rivals the Agab Modi'in and, of course, he didn't forget the local KGB man. For good measure he also dropped the story to another CIA man who he knew worked under the jurisdiction of the Directorate of Intelligence. Nice work indeed to get paid again for a story fed twice over to the same national organization! The stringer was experienced enough to realize how watertight were some of the various secret service departments — even operating from the same building. For the record, it just happened that this second CIA man was employed in the Office of Strategic Research, a sub-department that came under the umbrella of the Directorate of Intelligence.

Such are the ways in which bureaucratic machinery operates on the Western side of the Iron Curtain that first to act positively on the information received was Peter Hasler. Of course, he acted in this instance as a freelance dirty-tricks entrepreneur. When all the others had deliberated and procrastinated: minutes to ministers . . . section chiefs' memo-randa to departmental chiefs . . . recommended approval and official implementation received for authorization to act upon the information, et cetera, it was already far too late.

Fyodor Yankovsky had apparently defected and disappeared. To whom he had defected became one of the mysteries that bugged secret services and national police departments alike either side of the Iron Curtain.

★   ★   ★

Earlier George Brand realized he needed reliable professional help to pull it off. Someone who spoke Russian like a native. Most pro interpreters were out. Much too risky anyway for this kind of set-up. It was just too big for them! When they knew what was in the wind, they'd probably run, talk or both — no matter how inviting the bribe was. What's more, he didn't have time to find candidates like that who *might* fit the bill. He'd regretted not taking that technical Russian course way back. He spoke passable Spanish, German, French, Dutch, English, and, true, he did possess a smattering of Russian but only enough to get by in restaurants and hotels. It was not nearly good enough to risk fouling up the chance of a lifetime with problems of communication.

The potential trouble was that Yankovsky's English and German were only basic stuff. A little research into the Russian's background had told him this. He needed someone who spoke Russian like a native and who could be sure to get the unambiguous message through to Yankovsky . . .

When he thought about it, he knew there was only one other man known to him personally who fitted the bill as interpreter. Someone indoctrinated like himself into the art of dirty tricks who could more than pull his weight with the rest of the strong-arm covert stuff. Money wasn't any problem. There was more than enough potential gravy in this particular bowl to satisfy them both.

The man was Jake Kovas.

★ ★ ★

Even before his recent, undeclared, defection, Jake Kovas was not the most popular departmental member of the Agency. His immediate CIA supervisors had cause to reprimand him on several occasions over alleged brutality while seconded abroad on field assignments. He'd done little to hide his aggressive maleficent behaviour even from his colleagues — or his ex-wife. He'd been divorced five years back for the same offence. The New York judges took a less lenient view of agent Kovas's sadistic cruelties than his CIA superiors apparently did.

He'd been recruited from outside for service in Clandestine Services. It was there he found his forte. He was an original natural nasty if ever there was one. When he'd applied to join the Agency from the Bureau of Special Services (BOSS), his New York City Police Department colleagues were glad to help him on his way. He came highly recommended by a very senior CIA officer who had a lot of clout with someone in the Agency's Establishment. This senior officer had just cause to fear and, in turn, hate Kovas. He hated him with a vehemence beyond anything that he held for the official enemy — the KGB. Nobody of course knew this. The one redeeming feature about the transfer as far as the senior officer was concerned was that Kovas one day might meet his comeuppance more quickly in high-risk dirty-tricks; then life could be sweet again.

Meantime, Kovas had the goods on him. Those compromising pictures; he couldn't risk those ever being shown. It could spell the termination of his public-service career, ignominy and end his ambitions for high office. Kovas was a burden — the cross — he had to bear until . . .

He'd even intervened and saved Kovas from dismissal on two occasions. It had been possible because Kovas was tolerated for another reason. He spoke fluent Russian. Not many American-born CIA agents spoke really *fluent* Russian and could slip into a regional dialect at the drop of a hat and pass muster even to an expert's ear.

Kovas could.

This ability wasn't due to Kovas's excessive zeal for education (he'd once been nicknamed 'the Moron' by his ex-New York City Police Department colleagues), it was more an accident of birth. He was the offspring of Russian émigré parents, son of a proud mother and ex-teacher — one who wished her only child would never forget his roots. His otherwise broad New York ghetto accent, and the idiom that went with it, made him an incongruity at departmental meetings and raised many an eyebrow among the collegiate Ivy Leaguers who dominated the echelons of the Langley Building in Washington. That he was passed over for promotion time and time again by younger men with less service but with the right background and accents didn't bother Jake Kovas one little bit. He had the genius of a mobster. It was in the field at the sharp end of operations where you could cut yourself in on the gravy train whenever the opportunity offered itself. Get promotion behind a desk, and access to the gravy train stopped abruptly! If he had ambition, it was one born of greed to feather his nest whenever fate intervened.

When fate stepped in that morning in the guise of the transatlantic phone call from his old pal George, he couldn't get to Europe quickly enough.

★ ★ ★

Their plan had worked like a dream. With someone like Kovas in the deal with him, watching his back, the action wouldn't now go sour on him. He'd known Kovas's love of graft. It matched his own. They'd grafted together in the past; peanuts compared with this one. Even with this first pay-off they'd never have to work again. But even this now seemed like chicken-feed. Things were all relative. When the second part of his plan came off, they could both quietly slip out of circulation. He'd already made preparations for South America. If Nazi war criminals could disappear there, so could he and Kovas. They'd have to cover their tracks, but they never need be exposed as the front men.

He'd known beforehand that, potentially, Yankovsky would be a valuable prize. That's what it had all been about. But not *that* valuable. When they'd realized how valuable, they'd approached those contacts of his in the Middle East with a deal. Their backer had guaranteed them the sum paid in gold in a Swiss bank. The equivalent of five million in US greenbacks would be their share of the gravy for pulling it off. It was cheap at the price, and those boys in Beirut knew it. He should have asked for twenty million in gold. He'd sold himself and Kovas short. He'd been too eager to get hold of some real money. Life was full of regrets. Those contacts of his could easily stand that kind of traffic. Those principals he'd approached through his Baader-Meinhof connections had agreed it made good sense not to employ Arab faces directly in Norway. Arabs would stick out among the pale-faced Vikings like sore thumbs. He wondered how those Norwegian business colleagues of his were going to take it when he and Kovas double-crossed them . . .

Even Kovas still didn't know about his new money-making idea of testing the market elsewhere for the unique services of Fyodor Yankovsky. Not that he didn't trust Kovas, but that loose-mouthed West German stringer was still foremost in his memory . . . Now he'd disposed of him, that source wouldn't be giving any more trouble. That's how he'd got wind of Yankovsky's aberration, wasn't it! You had to be pragmatic in this life. He wouldn't let Kovas into his new plans until the time was ripe. Until then he and Kovas were comrades in arms with those friends in the Black September, working harmoniously together against the Jews. Those nebbishers in Tel Aviv were going to have a few sleepless nights, and all because of Yankovsky's deviate appetite for handsome, golden-haired boys! He'd need Kovas's help to pull off this second part of the op: to part Yankovsky from his Norwegian keepers.

To actually let Yankovsky press any buttons wasn't in his plans at all. He wanted no holocaust to interfere with his spending that loot — no chance of a World War III breaking out! He'd have to prove to the Russians, the CIA, the Israelis? — whoever it was bid the highest — he wasn't bluffing and could deliver. Meanwhile, it couldn't have worked out better. He now had Yankovsky safely on ice in a nice lonely spot where no one would find him.

There were still some organizational problems to be overcome, but if he and Kovas played their cards right — arranged the timing perfectly — they could slip away quietly after the lucky highest bidder dropped the gold in the right bank and took delivery of Yankovsky in situ. He and Kovas would have to make it look good, at least to the Black September people. If they ever suspected that he and Kovas had double-crossed them, they might come calling in South America.

9

Jim Hines, a career agent — basic grade — with an MIT PhD in physics and just two years' CIA service under his belt, was extra early to the office that morning. The call for a meeting with the Old Man had come at a quarter past midnight, via his immediate superior Larry Holmes.

It was just breaking daylight as he drove his Volkswagen into the partly wooded 125-acre tract just eight miles from downtown Washington. He was feeling a little apprehensive on two counts. He worked for the Foreign Missiles and Space Activities Centre under the umbrella of the Directorate of Science and Technology, and it wasn't that often he was included in dawn meetings to be chaired by William Carpenter, the 'supergrade' officer in charge of it. In fact, he'd only talked to Carpenter a handful of times since he'd joined the department after completing his basic training.

The Agency was a stickler for its chain-of-command protocol. Instructions, briefings, reports, brickbats or pats on the back were usually passed up or down the line respectively in single steps *unless it was a serious matter.* When facing the Old Man, he still felt like a rookie lieutenant about to have a levee with his divisional commander. And this was about the right analogy because in the Agency's pecking order, basic-grade career officers were about the lowest rung in the executive hierarchy while super-grades, in charge of the various Directorates, were rated 'generals'.

Astronomy and space travel had fascinated Jim ('Jimbo') Hines ever since junior school, but at high school he'd recognized his true bent was technological rather than academical. MIT had been his natural goal. He had the reputation now — in spite of his present lowly Agency status — of being somebody with a future. His subject at MIT had been electronics.

In his early days at MIT it was always

touch and go whether he'd later join NASA or opt for one of the big contractors working for NASA or other governmental agencies. The problem confronting Jim Hines and his contemporaries were the big cut-backs in the space programmes. He'd often regretted he'd been born two decades too late. He'd never given a single thought to a career in the CIA — not until he'd been approached one day on the campus of MIT by a well-groomed, hatchet-faced individual who introduced himself as Pat Haggerty.

Haggerty had flashed a card which looked very official and said he'd like to buy Jim Hines a hamburger and a Coke at the student commissary. Haggerty was a CIA recruiter; a scout, tout or huckster — depending on your point of view about such men. Had he, Jim Hines, ever thought of a Public-Service career? Good jobs these days, even for MIT PhDs, didn't grow on trees.

Haggerty was a persuasive man; that's why the CIA employed him in that role. Every man has some kind of forte;

Haggerty's was salesmanship. That day he sold the CIA to Jim Hines.

Mind you, after two years' Agency service under his belt, Jim Hines was an innocent no longer about his real recruiter. After listening to gossip — now part of his job — he'd realized his real recruiter was Jas McMasters, his old prof at MIT. Since joining the Agency — he himself didn't often refer to it as 'The Company' — he'd learnt that old Jas had been an OSS man during World War II and was now a talent spotter for the CIA. Hines was flattered his old prof had thought so much about him. He'd been flattered later by the fact he'd been finally selected as a trainee agent out of a batch of fifty other potential candidates. He'd have been less flattered to know that old Jas told the CIA that Hines was malleable material. The psychiatrists later agreed. In his favour Hines hadn't cared to bare his imagination too indiscreetly with those telling Rorschach tests, and he'd also done pretty well on the Gottschaldt Figures. Neither had he mentioned his interest in the poet Robert

Frost . . . All-American college boys with high IQs but with little real creative imagination — except for shapes and figures — were the very stuff of the Agency. After his indoctrination course (he came out front runner in the class graduation test) he'd actually enjoyed the field training — pistols, assault courses, unarmed combat, et cetera — down on 'The Farm' at Camp Peary in southern Virginia.

Now, after two years' service, the laminated plastic identity card that had to be on display at all times at Langley showed he was cleared for top security except for a 'bar-one' tag. Bar-one tags were reserved for officers at Directorate level. He could expect promotion any time; he already knew that on the files he'd been evaluated A-grade material after his probation period.

Hines's only problem was his young wife, Susie. Nowadays she got pretty tetchy about his cloak-and-dagger lifestyle which often spilled over into the domestic side. She had to know he was CIA, but that's all she knew and now often resented it. It was a CIA domestic syndrome that sooner or later all wives (and husbands) had to live with. In contrast to the big public corporations where wives were usually expected to openly participate in their husbands' careers, the CIA strictly forbade it. Mind you, they recognized an agent with an unhappy marriage was no asset to the Agency. For this reason there were some handsome wifely perks, and Susie Hines had enjoyed all those perks along with the other wives. Until little Abe came along four months back to clip her wings, she'd gone to Europe with her husband on several field missions. She was part of her husband's cover — which of course she'd suspected. At the Agency's expense she'd toured some of the capitals of Europe; bought top-fashion clothes in Paris; skied in Switzerland . . . She'd even seen the sights of Moscow. She'd learnt not to ask questions. Officially she knew her husband was supposed to be a research-scientist employee of Electronics Incorporated — a 'shell' establishment working on government contracts located just round the corner from Langley. The Agency actually used the building as a staff-overflow facility. Officially, Jim Hines had a desk in both establishments.

The real trouble had started with the arrival of little Abe; before that any discontent was only expressed in vague mutterings. When the phone call came through at quarter past midnight and immediately set little Abe screeching again, revolution festered. 'Jesus Christ! Why can't you find a normal job and be a regular nine-to-five husband for a change. Don't those bastards know you're a father now!'

She'd still been sulking when the alarm raised the roof at five and he'd got up and brewed himself some coffee. She'd not offered to get up and make him coffee or breakfast. He'd need to talk it out with her when he got back tonight. Maybe he should ask for a week off; he was overdue for some leave anyway. They could leave Abe with his mother and maybe visit West Palm Beach. She liked West Palm Beach. Maybe he'd even phone her at lunch-time and suggest a trip to Florida . . . Maybe tonight a candle-lit dinner for two at that French restaurant she liked if she could find a sitter. Maybe one of Holmes's daughters could sit for them. He didn't like frost in the bedroom.

10

Aboard the North Sea ferry, Kara Alstad and James Kerr lay together — relaxing in post-coital reverie. 'Have I now,' she murmured, 'established my bona fides to your entire satisfaction?'

'Let's say they'll pass muster for now, Miss Alstad, but I might need some more reassurance, later.' He remained straddled above her, their naked bodies face to face. Why not an encore tonight? he thought. He wanted to stay around anyway to find out more about this nosy bitch. In spite of her grand-passion performance just now, he still wasn't totally convinced she was *only* the person she claimed she was, but, anyway, let her go on thinking he had a trusting nature. Meantime, what better way of keeping an eye on her than sharing her sack! Field work could sometimes have its compensations.

Teasingly she nibbled at his earlobe. Yes, indeed — the thought reiterated itself

— field work did have compensations.

'Now, John Smith,' she said, 'shift your brute carcass and let me up. I have business in the Purser's Office. I think I should recover my life insurance *now*, just in case my friend there becomes over-curious. She made to push him away and, reluctantly, he rolled over on the narrow bunk to let her up. 'While I'm away, help yourself to a whisky. I shan't be long.'

He lay supine, watching her as she dressed; first in sheer undies and then in the trouser suit she'd worn earlier in the cafeteria. She had a fine body, he thought. Not skinny like those fashion models he'd sometimes gone to bed with; they looked like plucked birds, with a lattice of ribs, immature breasts, hollow belly and concave thighs. Kara Alstad had just enough flesh to make her curvy and interesting in the critical places.

She said, 'When I return, we must talk of more serious matters. Perhaps I shall bring a little something back from the cafeteria . . . ' and when she turned her head to look at him, he noted the mischievous glint in her eyes. 'Making love makes me hungry, and it's a long time until breakfast! Don't get bored while I'm away, John Smith.'

Before she left she came over to the bed and kissed him fully on the mouth.

'What was that for?' he asked.

'To seal our contract. Better than a handshake, don't you think?'

He agreed.

When she'd gone, he clambered lazily off the bed and walked over to click the latch on the door. Then he put on his shorts and poured himself a whisky.

Quite some girl, he reflected. Maybe he was just being *too* suspicious when he thought she might be playing games with him. If she *was*, she was a fine Method actress! That exhaustive joust was proof of it. The lingering image of her curvaceous body stayed sharply focused in his thoughts.

When he'd finished the first whisky, he poured himself another. This one he sipped more slowly; his thoughts stayed locked in agreeable post-coital reveries . . .

He was suddenly conscious of the

passage of time. It must be fifteen minutes since she'd left the cabin. An uneasiness crept surreptitiously into his gut.

Another five minutes ticked by. Then five more.

He raised himself from the bed and decided to dress.

When he'd finished dressing, he took a sheet of the ship's notepaper from the rack provided and scribbled a brief note in case he missed her. He wrote: *Got lonely and bored, so went in search of you,* he signed it *J.*

His first stop was down one deck to the forward vestibule where the Purser's Office was situated. She wasn't at the information counter. If she was still about, it could be she was inside the private office talking to that friend of hers? Maybe on the other hand she was now in the cafeteria standing in line to collect that night-food she'd promised?

At the cafeteria there was a long line at both checkouts, but no Kara Alstad.

Could be she was still in the Purser's Office or he'd missed her on the way back to the cabin? She'd probably gone back to her boat-deck cabin using the route via the stairs of the aft vestibule.

In cabin 64 there was still no sign of Kara Alstad. The note still lay untouched where he'd propped it up on the dressing-table. The unease in his gut now squirmed like a live eel.

Back to the Purser's Office. He'd throw caution to the winds. What the devil was Kara Alstad up to? Was that last kiss of hers something of a Judas kiss?

He tagged on behind a queue of three waiting at the information counter. When his turn came, he used the ploy: 'I have this friend aboard, see . . . ' At the mention of Kara Alstad's name there was no recognition on the face of the duty two-ringer giving out information. He dropped his eyes to consult a list. 'Cabin number 64, boat-deck.' Then he was already looking towards the next in line behind.

He needed time to think out his next move.

When he'd thought, he returned again to her cabin. Still no sign of her. Was she up front speaking to the captain explaining there was a dangerous fugitive masquerading as someone else aboard his ship? He walked up to the sun-deck where he could see a group of the ship's officers standing on the bridge. He didn't see anyone wearing four rings.

In turn he scoured the sun-deck, the boat-deck and then each of the lounges and bars. He even wandered through the waiter-service restaurant.

He explored the corridors of all the accommodation decks before rechecking the cafeteria and then finally back to cabin number 64.

He'd drawn a complete blank. It was as if Kara Alstad had disappeared from the ship.

It was now fifty minutes since she'd left him. Something was wrong. Was someone watching him? — someone playing a game of cat and mouse?

He left the cabin again and re-searched the whole ship in the areas where passengers were allowed. He doubled back along corridors, suddenly stopping and turning around to catch sight of anyone who might be following him.

In the end, exasperated, he gave up. It was now he wandered back to his own cabin.

When he pushed through the door, he finally came face to face with the person he'd been looking for. She took him by surprise, but she didn't acknowledge or make a grab at him. She didn't look nosy, inviting or the least bit comfortable. She lay fully clothed on his bed. Her blue eyes were staring vacantly into space. He'd seen enough corpses to realize by second glance Kara Alstad was stone-dead.

★ ★ ★

Earlier in the cafeteria Peter Hasler had positioned himself behind a pillar to watch Kara Alstad and her unknown male companion talk together. He'd seen her pass something across the table. A newsclip? Very mysterious. Their heads were bent close. Presently she got-up and started to walk out of the cafeteria. At a discreet distance he followed. He shadowed her all the way to her cabin. He noted the number was 64 and then returned to the cafeteria to watch the man she'd been talking to . . . Soon after the man also got up. He followed him down to the next deck and saw him enter cabin 101. He decided to wait in the corridor to see if the man came out again. The man was only inside a couple of minutes. When he passed him in the corridor, the man gave him a neutral level stare. He decided he probably hadn't seen this face before. He followed him all the way to Kara Alstad's cabin, saw him pause, knock on her door three times and then go inside.

What the devil were they up to?

He decided to wait and watch. Thirty minutes later Kara Alstad came out of her cabin alone. He followed her.

He intercepted her casually at the end of the corridor. 'Ah, Miss Alstad . . . ' He was suave and polite. 'I thought I saw you come aboard. Now I've bumped into you again, I've been having second thoughts about that interview you requested. Remember — last time we met? 'Americans in Exile' I think you called your series . . . As you remarked yourself, a little free publicity never hurt anyone's business . . . Say we step along to my cabin. We could have a drink together while we talk . . . '

★   ★   ★

She hadn't expected to meet Hasler face to face at the end of the corridor. She hadn't expected him to turn on the charm either. After all, he'd given her a very positive brush-off both times she'd approached him previously on the subterfuge of writing him into that Exile series. When she'd left Kerr inside her cabin, all she wanted to do was to contact Felix again in Oslo and tell him she'd now established 'contact' with the Englishman and, what's more, they might have to revise their assessment of what sort of game he and his late Norwegian companion were playing in Hasler's affairs. Now she'd been diverted by the American and he was inviting her to his cabin. This was too good an opportunity to miss. She'd go along for the ride — not however the kind she'd taken James Kerr on! Some things you did for your adopted country without fuss . . . but in no way did she fancy Hasler in bed.

When a few moments later she stepped over the threshold of cabin 101, she'd no way of knowing it was the cabin of the man whose fresh seed she carried . . .

11

It was a visibly angry William Carpenter who chaired the meeting he'd called for 6 a.m. on the fourth floor of the Langley Building. Apart from Jim Hines also present were Hines's immediate superior Larry Holmes and three senior-grade officers — Kerry Doyle, Sam Bentley and George Willard. All, including their chief, were science PhDs — the minimum qualification for employment within the Directorate of Science and Technology. Carpenter, who'd once been a full-time professor of physics at Northwestern, had, in addition, a DSc plus several foreign honours. He was an ex-Harvard man. Sam Bentley and George Willard held down part-time associate professorships at Georgetown; they were graduates of Princeton and Yale respectively. Kerry Doyle was also an ex-Yale man. For good reason the Science and Technology Directorate were known as the Ivy

League egg-heads, and with it went a connotation — especially from their colleagues in the Directorate of Intelligence — that wasn't entirely flattering to their image.

'Jimbo' Hines was the most junior of all the career officers present. When he heard the name Fyodor Yankovsky, he knew the reason why he'd been invited along to the Old Man's breakfast show.

He could barely believe his ears . . . Yankovsky had defected, then apparently gone missing! So the Old Man said, anyway. Yankovsky had been part of his scientific brief since joining the CIA. He and Holmes had shared the job of shadowing him at all the international scientific congresses the Russian attended. It was a shock to discover this outstanding technologist was a homosexual. But then neither his brief nor Holmes's had ever been to follow the man beyond his bedroom door — or to analyse his private life. It wasn't what they were there to do. Their job had been as scientific *agents provocateurs*. It had long been suspected that Yankovsky himself was a part-time

KGB man. As garrulous, over-friendly Western scientists they'd played a double role: firstly, to glean between the lines what they could about Yankovsky's military research work inside the Soviet Union; and secondly, as innocent messengers of scientific and technological disinformation to confuse the KGB and GRU. Their second role was as important as the first — probably more so. After all, it had been the Russians who'd started the *dezinformatsiya* war and ran a special department inside the KGB to handle it.

If a leak from the Russians hadn't confirmed that Yankovsky was gay, Hines wouldn't have believed it. For one thing he didn't look or act like any of those gays he'd seen openly flaunting their deviancy on the West Coast or that guy who'd once tried to proposition him in Times Square . . . So Yankovsky was numbered among those 'One in Twenty'! As an epithet it had stuck in his mind ever since reading that paperback of the same title. Personally, that book had been more revelatory than Einstein's *The Meaning of Relativity* . . . Until he'd read *One in Twenty*, he'd only had a pretty vague idea of what homosexuals did — to each other!

According to what the statistics said, one human being out of twenty was afflicted with the curse — men *and* women. In idle moments among company, he'd often since played the game of trying to spot the jokers in the pack. He'd wondered about his colleagues in the CIA. Rumour had it some departments were loaded. How did they get by all that psychiatric screening? Then, homos, he'd learnt since joining the Agency, were pretty good actors — just like the converse was true that actors were often homos . . . Looking round the table, he wondered if any of the present company had a penchant for buggery . . . The sight or sound of that word still curdled in his naïve, all-American, wholesome-boy brain. If any of those round the table were gay, they kept it under wraps. He knew for certain that Larry Holmes wasn't bent — at least not that way. They'd been in the field together, and in the field you get to know a lot about guys. Holmes was happily married with a couple of kids, but he did have a wandering eye and weakness for young blonde Fraüleins just out of pigtails with big tits and shapely asses. If Holmes was any kind of deviant, it was strictly a Playboy-style deviancy for macho-male normalcy — the kind when diagnosed by the CIA medics passed you through with flying colours and sighs of relief from Establishment.

At the recent conference held in the Hague, it had been Holmes, alone, who'd attended. Hines this time had remained back in Langley to complete the Section's three-monthly evaluation bulletin on Soviet ballistic missiles required by the front office. It was one of those regular updating paperwork chores that came up all too often.

Hines, an obliging underling who had proved himself a dab hand at composing bureaucratic gobbledygook since joining the department, volunteered to stay behind to complete it. He'd been thinking of Susie and her recent bitchiness about his absences from base.

Holmes, sitting next to him, now realized he'd got a lot of egg on his face after the Old Man dropped his bombshell with news of Yankovsky's defection. The Old Man had paused to see its effects on Holmes. Holmes, caught out, immediately admitted he'd 'defected' himself from the back end of the conference before Yankovsky had gone. Hines guessed right that his superior had left for a cross-border assignation with one of his blonde Fraüleins. Holmes's spontaneous cover-story, delivered extempore and somewhat shakily to those now seated round the table, was he'd taken off to Bonn to check on a promising lead from one of the Agency's part-time local agents.

The Old Man looked grim. There was bound to be a departmental inquest on this one. Someone might decide to check back with that part-time agent he was supposed to have contacted. Holmes himself now recognized he might be caught flagrante — with his metaphorical if not his literal pants firmly round his ankles.

' . . . So the f'ing bastard's just slipped through our fingers,' concluded Carpenter with an emphatic, disgusted tone and falling back on vocabulary picked up at the same time as his World-War-II campaign medals and unmodified since. He'd just finished acquainting his supernumeraries round the table with the facts of the situation as he'd heard it from his opposite number in the Directorate of Intelligence.

Holmes's expression was one of suitable chagrin. He wisely opted to remain quiet. He left it to Kerry Doyle to pick up an obvious loose end. 'But you say, chief, that one of the boys in Strategic Research passed on the rumour about Yankovsky's 'state of health' eight weeks back . . . Why, for Christ's sake, wasn't our Directorate told? Surely those cretins upstairs would know we'd be interested in that kind of spicy, hot gossip? . . . '

'They didn't tell us because they were hogging it for themselves, as per usual. I've just learned the inner top brass of the Forty Committee has been tossing around a proposal for some covert action apropos Yankovsky for the past four weeks . . . They'd planned on asking me for our opinion at tomorrow's meeting . . . '

'After the bird had flown, Jesus!' exclaimed Bentley, getting himself into the act of universal disgust. 'All this inter-directorate rivalry must be a real giggle for the KGB. If it wasn't for the fact they've got some egg on their faces in this one too, they'd be splitting their sides . . . Any chance the KGB are giving out with a forked tongue? Remember how they booby-trapped us before with all that razzmatazz about their lost nuclear sub in the Pacific? . . . '

'No, they know the Agency wouldn't fall for apple sauce like that again,' suggested Willard.

'You're probably right about that, George,' concurred Carpenter. 'I think this one has the taste of genuine homebaked crust.'

'The Forty Committee are always lousing things up,' said Doyle. 'They've acted like a bunch of pussy-footing old ladies ever since Hawkeye departed.'

'Let's all skip the recriminations bit,' suggested Carpenter. Holmes's face suddenly brightened at this news. After a pause, Carpenter, now wearing a calculating look, glanced at each round the table. 'We've still got a chance to do something off our own bat on this one. Maybe we can come out of it smelling of roses if we play our cards right . . . '

' . . . and show 'em we're not just a bunch of absent-minded eggheads,' chipped in the bald-domed Willard with a grin. Willard was known to be a close personal friend of Carpenter's.

'But we can't act unilaterally without prior approval of the Forty Committee . . . Or can we . . . ?' said Bentley, his voice suddenly trailing off as he caught a gleam in Carpenter's eye.

'You're catching on fast, Sam, but we're not going to act unilaterally. We haven't the wherewithal for a start . . . But we do have friends in the Pentagon who have . . . '

Hines recognized by the drift of his chief's conversation he was about to become party to a new departmental intrigue and inwardly thrilled to the prospect of it. At a distance he'd always admired Carpenter's legendary cool nerve and powerful intellect. Tall, silver-haired, with the air of a wise but iron-willed veteran senator, he had a charismatic quality. After all, you didn't become head boy of a CIA Directorate for nothing! The man was supposed to have an IQ rating of 150 and was reported to be quite a performer in the upper echelons of Langley politics. It was a fact often discussed in the Agency that since Hawkeye himself had left the Forty Committee, Carpenter was one of the few remaining red-bloods left in the brass of the Agency with any power. Some said he had ambition to become the CIA's next Director and had a lot of pull with the Republican presidental nominee. Hines didn't doubt any of the gossip he'd heard; in spite of the jocular familiarity Carpenter seemed to encourage in his supernumeraries, he sensed all those round the table were a little afraid and in awe of their chief.

Carpenter eyed his audience speculatively from under his hooded lids. 'We'll call this little co-opted exercise of ours 'Project Recovery' — for reasons which I'll specify shortly.' He glanced at his watch and then reached for the green telephone by his right hand. 'You can tell Commander Morrison to come in now, please.'

A few seconds later a full commander wearing the gold braid of the USN took his place in a vacant chair next to Carpenter. Everyone recognized the newcomer was a member of Naval Intelligence and it was quite unnecessary for the fact to be spelt out.

' . . . Commander Morrison is totally in the picture, gentlemen, as far as I've already explained matters. As you may imagine, our Navy Intelligence friends share our common interest in Yankovsky . . . I am also led to believe they have their own problem with the Pentagon brass . . . ' Carpenter paused for his mild joke to be appreciated.

' . . . I won't mince words, gentlemen, it has been agreed between us to attempt recovery of one of the Soviet's Silent Men missiles now probably lying at the bottom of the Oslofjord . . . '

He paused again, and his glance swept round the table to gauge how the news had registered on each of his super-numerary audience.

Willard was the first to comment. ' . . . Without prior approval of the Forty Committee?'

'Definitely *without*,' smiled back Carpenter.

'Covert action?' asked Kerry Doyle.

'Very covert,' replied Carpenter and focused towards the commander.

Morrison, taking his cue, cleared his throat. 'Two months ago we were tipped off by US Navy Global Surveillance that something odd had occurred during a mission of a Kalinin-class Soviet nuclear-powered sub which had penetrated the Oslofjord, and during the course of which it performed some rather unconventional manoeuvres. We believe these odd manoeuvres were the specific instances she purposely ejected several Silent Men missiles and their launching pods on the seabed . . . We think we know their precise locations within a few metres. I would remind you, gentlemen, that the United States has never yet recovered an intact Soviet long-range nuclear missile.

In this instance we have a unique opportunity to rectify that significant lacuna in our knowledge of Soviet weaponry. There are risks; but if our objective is successful, it could give us inestimable advantages over the Soviets during the next decade . . . Even our politicians might eventually be grateful to us . . . '

There was muted laughter.

'Just a minute, Commander,' cut in Bentley. 'I agree with both you and the chief. We *could* all come out of this smelling of roses if we grabbed the goods, but what about all those highly sophisticated electronic booby-traps we've been hearing about that could be attached to those missiles? How do we get round that problem? Or is it the navy thinks the Russians are bluffing so we won't go poaching?'

Morrison turned towards Carpenter. Carpenter nodded and took over the reins. 'That's one possibility, Sam. Mind you, they could be telling the truth . . . At worst we might decide it's only prudent to go in for a quick stand-off look-see.

Whether we attempt a definite heist would all depend . . . ' He looked in turn round the table as if to prompt and solicit the answer he already knew himself.

Only Hines reacted. 'If we could locate Yankovsky, sir . . . '

' . . . That's *precisely* what I had in mind myself,' chipped in Carpenter wearing his avuncular look.

★ ★ ★

When the meeting broke up one hour later, Hines, immediately phoned his wife from Carpenter's own outer sanctum. He anticipated an explosion. He got one. 'Wha'd'ya mean you're not coming home for a few days! . . . You can't do this to us, Jimbo! What the hell's going on down there at Langley? Tell those bastards you work for you've got a wife and kid . . . responsibilities . . . Important you say! I bet it is. More important than me or Abe! . . . Sure, I'm sure. How would you take it, buster, if I phoned you at the office and told you I was just hopping off on a mystery tour? . . . '

He'd let her rant on. Work off steam. He could appreciate her point of view. But damn it! This was his job. When the brass said take off, you took off, without questions. The Old Man had a point of view, too. No one in the CIA knew Yankovsky better than he and Holmes. They'd talked to the guy dozens of times, swopped pleasantries and quietly dropped him a lot of disinformation hocus. Yankovsky was believed to be holed up — hiding someplace in Norway. He had to be if he *was* going to control those Silent Men missiles. If anyone could persuade Yankovsky to come over and roost in the States, it was he or Holmes. His Russian wasn't that hot but a lot better than Holmes's, and it was good enough if he could make contact with the help of the Norwegian Secret Service who'd promised co-operation in the op. His job then would be to find out some of the technicalities of those missiles and spell out the rewards of United States citizenship and the very generous life-insurance protection offered by the Agency . . . Maybe even help him find a compatible homosexual mate. The last thought still stuck in his craw. That had been Sam Bentley's idea. It made him feel more like some kind of pimp — instead of an agent empowered with a critical life-or-death mission.

12

Without disturbing Kara Alstad's corpse, Kerr could plainly see how she'd met her death. She wasn't exactly a pretty sight. She wore a full set of nasty bruises round her throat. Her lolling tongue had already taken on a deep shade of royal purple. When he touched her skin, it was chill. He guessed she must have come to his cabin soon after she'd left her own. What about that note in the Purser's Office? Now he didn't believe a word of it. There'd never been such a note!

What the blazes was she doing in *his* cabin anyway? Who the devil had killed her? Why had she been killed? And why in *his* cabin? The questions rattled in his brain like a burst from a submachine-gun.

He clicked the latch of the cabin door. Then he picked up her shoulder-bag. He opened it and shook out the contents on the carpeted floor. On the way to the floor something recognizably lethal dropped out.

First he rummaged among the paper debris just in case — his second thoughts on the subject — she might after all have collected a note from the Purser's Office before her killer intercepted her. If she had, there was no sign of any such note, nor, for that matter, was there any sign of the Dutch newspaper clip she'd shown him earlier in the cafeteria. With his own eyes he'd seen her slip it back into her shoulder-bag.

He examined her shoulder-bag contents piece by piece. First that lethal piece. Question: What was a journalist doing with a 'two-five 6-shot pocket Bauer automatic? Self-protection, of course; that was the easy part of the answer. Self-protection from whom? He couldn't make progress on that one except it proved her killer had taken her unawares before she could use it.

He turned his attention to the rest of the contents: Her cabin ticket; a landing-card already made out for Kristiansand/ Oslo; press card; mini-diary; American

Express travel cheques; Bank of Norway domestic cheque-book; combined purse and billfold well stacked with sterling pounds, US greenbacks and norske kroner; powder; lipstick; anti-perspirant; face cream; tissues . . . finally her passport.

The passport was a Norwegian one. Her name and the basic facts she'd told him checked out. Occupation: journalist; then reckoning from the date of birth written in the front — aged 26. Next he scanned the inside pages. No recent visas, but lots of various European in-and-out immigration stamps. What caught his eye were two recent in-and-out West German dates and then two more Dutch ones. They tallied with the dates in his own passport he'd carried in the name of Philip Gill . . . He'd interchanged those pages so his James Kerr passport showed the correct in-and-out date stamps.

Coincidence was it these dates tallied with his and Olaf's? It confirmed she — possibly others? — had been shadowing him and Olaf through West Germany and then Holland.

In the pages of her mini-diary were unspecified lists of phone numbers . . . Norwegian? European? Routine? He skipped into the dated pages and then saw it . . . In Norwegian it said: 'Peter Hasler — *forsök å intervjue ham?*' Why did she want to interview Hasler? As a journalist? Now it hit him! *Hasler!* of course, she could have been tailing the American — not Olaf or him. Or was she tailing all three of them? Could it be she was an undercover agent of the Norwegian Secret Service — the PO[1]? Were the PO independently onto Hasler's activities in Norway because of his involvement with those neo-Nazis? — and Kara Alstad in the guise of a free-roaming journalist was his shadow? That scenario had the ring of truth. Beyond that he didn't make progress because finding Hasler's name in her diary displaced all other thoughts . . . Hasler, of course, had tumbled to the fact she was tailing him and killed her. Hasler must have seen Kara Alstad and

---

[1] Full title: Politiets Overvakningstjeneste

him talking in the cafeteria . . . Hasler had even followed him down to check the number of his cabin . . . Hadn't he spotted the American lurking outside after he'd brushed his teeth . . . Hasler had seen Kara Alstad leave her cabin . . . On some pretence he'd enticed her into cabin 101 to kill her . . . Now Hasler would be waiting somewhere near by to see what her travelling companion would do about it when he found the corpse . . . *It spelt out Hasler was definitely onto him.*

He slipped her 'two-five Bauer into his own pocket, returned the rest of the things into the shoulder-bag and moved over to take another look at her corpse. He paid particular attention to her hands. Then, having satisfied himself on one point, he locked the door behind him and went in search of her killer.

★ ★ ★

Down the corridor Peter Hasler was now more certain in his mind . . . So that Norwegian journalist bitch he'd just strangled did know *something*. Wasn't that newsclip he'd fished out of her shoulder-bag evidence enough! His sixth sense had proved him right again. Did she know his real name was Brand? The problem now was deciding *how* much she'd known and others *knew*. Had she any connection with Solberg? Was she working with him? How much had she told that tall stranger she'd been talking to in the cafeteria?

According to the Purser's Office — when he checked there — the occupant of cabin 101 was a James Kerr — an Englishman? — but he couldn't quite see yet how a limey came into it.

Whatever, this limey was his immediate danger now. He'd seen Kara Alstad show him the clip. There was no quick way of finding out how much he knew. No choice but to get rid of him as he'd got rid of that bitch. A nice clean job; no incriminating bloodstains; no shooting — nothing to implicate him directly. But how was he going to take this limey unawares? He was a big guy. He'd be no pushover like that female — especially

now he'd found her body in his cabin
. . . A stroke of genius enticing that nosy
bitch into the limey's cabin. He'd killed
two birds with one stone. It proved she
didn't know too much about this limey
— otherwise she'd have known about his
cabin, wouldn't she?

How would this guy Kerr play it now?
Raise hell like he didn't know what was
going on? The way he would react would
be the key to how much he knew and
how much he'd been involved with that
bitch. So he'd wait and see how the
limey handled it. If he was on a covert
op, he'd not be raising Cain or any hue
and cry. Whatever, he'd be in a hell of a
dilemma to know what to do for the
best. All the pressure would be on him
now. He'd been *almost* certain there'd
been no sign of recognition in the
limey's eyes when they'd met in the
corridor. He couldn't have disguised that
— not unless he was a bloody good
actor. Yet he couldn't be one hundred
per cent sure . . . First he'd go up to the
bar and have a few drinks. He needed a
drink. If Kerr *did* know who he was, he

might come calling himself . . . While he waited in the bar, he'd think of ways of getting rid of him before morning without fuss.

13

Kerr found the American sitting alone at a table in the Long Bar in the ship's forward lounge nursing a half-empty glass. He sat down on a stool by the counter, his back to Hasler. In the panoramic mirror behind the bottle display he could see the American watching him. He ordered a double whisky and kept Hasler's reflection in his sights.

Presently he saw the American knock back the remains of his drink and stroll over to the bar counter. All the stools were empty except the one occupied by himself. Hasler chose the sixth stool to the left and ordered a bourbon.

On impulse he decided to try a game of bluff and keep the initiative over the American. Wasn't *Audaci favet fortuna* the motto of his old regiment? The American might be taken off his guard. Another thing, he wanted an excuse to get to close quarters for a good look at him.

'Bill Pately . . . ' said Kerr, playing theatre and addressing the American. 'It *is* Bill Pately, isn't it? You old son of a gun. I wasn't sure when we passed in the corridor earlier. How long is it, ten years?' Kerr swung himself off his own stool and then sat down on the one to the right of Hasler and thrust his hand out.

He saw the American blink, involuntarily put his hand out to meet his own and then almost immediately start to withdraw it again. 'Wrong guy, bud,' Hasler said dismissively. 'The name's Hasler. I've never met you before in my life.'

'Really!' exclaimed Kerr, now caught up in his thespian game. He'd caught hold of the American's retreating hand and gripped it. It was the hand of a professional killer. One of those hands had just throttled Kara Alstad . . . 'Well,' said Kerr, 'that just goes to show how memory plays tricks. I could have sworn you were my old chum Pately. You're sure? . . . '

'Of course I'm sure,' said the American with irritation growing in his voice.

Kerr was eyeing Hasler at close range now. He wanted to be sure he was Kara Alstad's killer. The long arm of coincidence sometimes had a nasty habit of reaching out. He was searching particularly for a very distinct Sherlock Holmesian clue . . .

The American looked a lot different to those urban guerrillas he consorted with. He was clean-shaven, dark-complexioned — probably a twice-a-day shaver; bushy-browed, short-cut hair, styled and neatly parted. He wore a well-pressed, charcoal-grey business suit; a white shirt with a starched collar; a subdued, expensive silk tie. A man who took pains and pride in his appearance? Why then that fresh crimson scratch mark just behind his right ear and that spot of blood from the same scratch staining his collar neckline? Kerr realized they'd both be invisible to the American unless he twisted his head and noticed them in the bar mirror.

Nicked himself, had he, while shaving earlier?

But he wouldn't nick himself on the skin *behind* the ear, would he? Something else might though. Those long fingernails of Kara Alstad might just have nicked him *once* as she'd briefly fought for her life! Back in the cabin he'd noticed there'd been a definite trace of blood under the nail of her right index finger. He'd made a point of examining her fingers closely.

The long arm of coincidence could be damned.

Kerr said, 'Well . . . I really could have sworn you were Pately. You're his double then . . . ' He finished his whisky, and said, 'Cheerio, old chap. I think I'll now take a spin on the upper deck for a little air. Stuffy in here,' and he walked out of the bar.

Outside, Kerr broke into a run. Taking the steps three at a time, to the astonished glances of other passengers, he mounted the main vestibule stairs leading to the boat-deck. When he reached the boat-deck, he immediately immersed himself in a pool of shadow out of sight, back from the main walkway.

He waited only a couple of minutes

before the American came hurrying by, wearing busy eyes. The fact that he'd followed him up on deck now convinced him Hasler was tailing him and probably at first opportunity intended to kill him just as he'd killed Kara Alstad. Whatever, with Hasler his cover was now blown. The words of the general echoed through his brain again. *Once your cover as an agent is blown, you are no longer of use to the SOC.*

He decided it was time for this ex-CIA villain to get some of his own treatment. That would solve the problem, and on the way there were scores to settle.

From his hiding-place he watched Hasler move down towards the stern end and then, with one final glance back, start to climb the aft companion way leading up to the open sports deck. A few seconds later he'd disappeared from view.

For the next half minute Kerr sat tight waiting and watching — just in case the American doubled back. Then, when he decided he wasn't going to do that, he left his hiding-place, walked swiftly down the length of the boat-deck and stole up the same companion way he'd seen Hasler disappear. A few steps below the sports deck he stopped short for a *shufti*. He'd learned in the army not to go barging into things half-cocked, for that was the way to get your fool head blown right off. Stand, look and listen, let the situation resolve itself . . .

The sports deck was bathed in darkness. An unseasonal chill North Sea breeze cut in from the east; the deck was deserted of passengers. Above, a couple of ships' lights glowed subdued. To the west, low cloud covered the pale ghost of a first-quarter moon.

When his eyes adapted to the semi-darkness, he distinctly glimpsed the frontal outline of a man waiting on the edge of the shadows.

Hasler had laid an ambush for his killing-spot; he now expected the Englishman to walk into it.

Kerr silently retraced his steps down the companion way to the boat-deck and then moved swiftly along towards the bow end of the ferry where he knew another companion way led up. When he reached it, he cautiously mounted it and, on reaching the sports deck again, reconnoitred the situation. The American was still there in the shadows apparently still watching towards the stern end. Stealthily Kerr moved forwards — keeping inside the weak moon shadows cast by the canvas awnings.

Kerr estimated he was just less than two yards short of the concealed form when he decided to charge him. He suddenly jackknifed his body at hip level and at the same time drove his head forwards to ram his target.

He was already committed and moving horizontally when he sensed he was a shade off line. Damn the man! The American had shifted his stance slightly. He'd probably heard a sound behind him and had already begun to turn to look towards it.

Instead of Kerr butting him in the small of the back as intended, his head collided with the softer pelvic regions. At the same time Kerr saw something catch the faint light and flash past and miss his head by a whisker. He felt the wind of it as it struck his shoulder. From the impact of the blow on his collar-bone, instinct told him it might be the long barrel of an automatic pistol. He knew from experience the long barrel of an auto pistol could be a very effective truncheon at close quarters.

As Hasler staggered under the momentum of the surprise impact, then lost his footing and toppled backwards, Kerr grabbed towards his falling body to search out and pin his gun arm. He found the arm but didn't succeed in pinning it down.

Locked in each other's grip, they began to roll about the deck. Hasler, Kerr noted, was very strong; his hands gripped like steel claws, but he instinctively felt he'd have the edge on the American in open rough-house combat. His greater weight and height would give him advantage. He decided to take a chance. He suddenly released his grip on Hasler's wrist, snatched at him again and in one continuous movement whipped him round through one hundred and eighty degrees. Momentarily he released his hold again and regripped him by his jacket lapels. After a split-second pause, Kerr hauled the American to his feet and, wrenching violently downwards, dragged his jacket over his shoulders, locking Hasler's arms. It was a standard drill he'd been taught at the SOC combat school to immobilize an armed man. He must have rehearsed and practised those basic movements a hundred times before. The American was now effectively incarcerated in a strait-jacket.

'Now, Mr bloody Hasler,' hissed Kerr, 'what have you got to say for yourself?' The American continued to struggle, but he couldn't break out of the lock on his arms. Kerr brought his knee up smartly and jabbed it hard into Hasler's back. 'Drop that pistol and then start talking or I'll break your bloody spine. I want to know why you killed Solberg and Kara Alstad . . .'

Kerr heard the pistol hit the deck with a clatter. At the same instant Hasler did something Kerr didn't anticipate. He drove back with his right elbow, hard into Kerr's chest, and immediately broke free of the lock on his upper arms. Like a skink shedding its skin to the claws of an enemy, the American wriggled his arms free and started to pull away. Kerr instantly dropped the empty jacket and hurled himself forwards, grabbing Hasler round the waist in a full-blooded tackle. Locked together, they crashed heavily against the ship's railing.

Recovering equilibrium almost simultaneously, each embraced the other — their hands frantically searching out and grasping like two equally matched wrestlers striving to find an advantage hold. Kerr suddenly felt the American go limp and was surprised by it. He was caught off guard for a fleeting second and, before he knew it, Hasler's killer hands were round his neck, pincering into his windpipe in a two-handed grip. As his thumbs pressed home and probed more deeply, Kerr flexed his neck muscles to maintain his breathing and began to pummel away at Hasler's body with his fists.

Rat-like, the American hung on tenaciously as Kerr, driven by pain, continued to flail away at him, using Hasler's body as a punch-ball. Kerr had never experienced such a constriction round his throat. Catherine-wheels spun in his head. Under the haze of pain he realized that Hasler would strangle him if he didn't soon break free of his two-handed bear-grip.

Dredging up all his remaining strength, Kerr staggered to his feet, dragging the American up with him. Then, lifting him off the ground, he bounced him hard back against the metal railing.

Still Hasler's hands wouldn't let go. Again and again Kerr lifted him and dashed him against the railing. Soon he lost count. His brain was hazed. Then, when he felt himself sinking, Kerr heard something snap. The American let out a soft, low moan, and his hands fell away from Kerr's throat. Hasler now seemed to arch backwards; he kept on arching, almost floating, then silently curved into space.

It was not until Kerr heard the faint splash below he comprehended the American had fallen overboard.

Kerr caught his breath, straightened his tie and jacket and then checked around the deck to see if anyone had witnessed the action. He concluded there'd been no bystanders.

He found the American's jacket and then the pistol. It was a 9mm Browning automatic with a hand-checkered walnut stock and a full clip of 13 shots. He unscrewed the silencer, slipped it in his pocket for safekeeping and tucked the pistol down his waistband.

Now he concentrated on Hasler's jacket. He rummaged in the pockets and in turn pulled out what was probably a passport, a leather billfold and a small stiff envelope. It was too dim to identify the items with certainty. For the moment he stuffed them unseen inside his own pocket.

He didn't find anything else and he walked over to the lee-side railing and tossed the jacket overboard.

Back in his cabin Kara Alstad's corpse lay undisturbed. The sickening sweet smell of death now pervaded the whole place. He was totally exhausted and felt like retching up. He was almost tempted to steal along to Kara Alstad's cabin to pick up the rest of that whisky, but he resisted.

He reached into his pockets to satisfy his curiosity about the items he'd removed from the American's jacket. One was a passport made out in the name of Peter Hasler — obviously a forgery, but an excellent one ... The leather object was a billfold and then there was the envelope. He ignored the contents of the billfold and explored the envelope ... Inside was a bundle of photographs. Flipping through them quickly, he realized they were two photographic subjects and several duplicate copies of each. One was of two nude males caught flagrante in an homosexual act — a youth about fifteen and a man about forty. It was like a frame of montage clipped direct from an action film. The man had features like that of an East European. Kerr was sure he vaguely recognized him but couldn't give him a name. The same man was the principal subject of a second photograph.

He'd been photographed sitting in a chair with his hands firmly bound in front of him.

What the hell had Hasler been up to?

14

At number 2 Dzerzhinsky Square, Colonel Stephan Zigel sat in his office drumming his fingers on his desk top; the earlier set puzzled frown now easing from his brow. In front of him lay the open, bulging file of Fyodor Yankovsky. Alongside it were several decoded cables: two, especially, interested him — one received from the Soviet Embassy in the Hague, the other routed from the Embassy in Oslo . . .

During the preceding twelve hours the colonel had read and sifted through Yankovsky's file half a dozen times. The overflowing ashtray and the two empty vodka-bottles, lying as dead men in his trash-basket, were visible reminders of his marathon session to rebrief himself before attending the morning's meeting with the general.

In spite of consuming two quarts of a brand vodka known as 'extra' (a

Rolls-Royce product of Soviet distilleries) plus two packs of British export Senior Service (procured for him via one of KGB's undercover plants at the British Embassy and which he preferred to all local cigarettes) he was remarkably clear-headed.

Several points now seemed resolved to him at least; and when his duty clerk rapped on the door of his private office to remind him it was time for the meeting, he quickly gathered up the papers and then briskly set off down the corridor to the briefing-room located in the annex of the general's own suit of offices.

General Kostantin Kerbel's face was impassive as he took his seat at the head of the table. Colonel Zigel sat immediately to his left. Others round the table included another full colonel and two majors — named respectively: Kulik, Sverchkov and Razin. It was Major Razin — the general's office assistant — who was delegated to take the minutes of the proceedings.

Colonel Zigel's gaze fell on the three portraits adorning the walls of the briefing-room. The first two were the inevitable pictures of Marx and Lenin. Cliché wall-decoration throughout every public building in the Soviet Union. What did his counterparts in the CIA have to stare at during idle moments in the Langley Centre in Washington? . . . Thomas Jefferson? George Washington? Abraham Lincoln? . . . That thought always intrigued him. Perhaps he'd never know. The third portrait hanging in the room was Feliks Edmundevich Dzerzhinsky, the founder of the Soviet Secret Service, who'd confiscated the grey stone building of the All Russian Insurance Company in 1918. He mused over the changes it must have seen through the years — from Cheka to GPU, then NKVD, MVD and now the Committee for State Security — the KGB.

The colonel's eyes momentarily alighted on the shelf of honour — the trophies and shields containing the names of the champion sportsmen of Lubyanka. His gaze locked onto the swimming-shield and, although from the distance of the table he couldn't read it, he knew his name had been inscribed on it for the past five years . . . 'S Zigel: 1500 and 3000 metres swimming-champion'. After literature and music, swimming was his great relaxation in time of stress.

No one else round the table, except Colonel Zigel, had yet seen the cables from the Hague and Oslo. Hopefully both were his trump cards for this morning's meeting — his face-savers . . . Zigel had known Yankovsky well. He was Yankovsky's control, and it was under the colonel's advice and subsequent patronage that one of Russia's top scientists had been recruited as a part-time KGB agent on his trips abroad to attend scientific congresses. When Yankovsky had apparently defected, Colonel Zigel had immediately lost face with his general superior and professional kudos with his equals and inferiors at Lubyanka. Past glories were forgotten. As critics judge actors, the KGB hierarchy judged you on your performances. As an effective member of the KGB you were only as good as your current rating. Colonel Zigel's rating, apropos Yankovsky, was at this moment at nadir.

As Zigel glanced round the table at the faces of his KGB comrades, he saw unmistakable signs of *Schadenfreude* reflected in their expressions. He smiled inwardly to himself. *Just wait, comrades.* The general coughed; a sign for Colonel Zigel to start bringing him up to date with events and developments — if any — over the past few hours respecting Fyodor Yankovsky.

'Our comrade scientist did not after all defect in Holland,' he announced matter-of-factly, 'he has probably been abducted . . . ' Zigel paused to let the impact of his news sink in and also to watch the face of his arch-rival for high office — Colonel Matvei Kulik — who was seated on the opposite side of the table.

Zigel saw Kulik blink but remain discreetly silent; it was left to the general to repeat aloud, ' . . . probably abducted?' and leave an intentional big question-mark behind it.

'Yes, comrade General, probably abducted. There must still be an element

162

of doubt, of course, but I am now ninety-five per cent sure he did not defect to the Palestinians of his own free will.'

'Only ninety-*five* per cent sure, comrade?' chipped in Kulik sarcastically. He just couldn't hold back his snide remark.

Zigel ignored it.

The general said curtly, 'Reasons, comrade.'

Without speaking, Zigel passed him the two decoded cables.

There was silence for several minutes while the general perused them both. Then he looked up at Zigel; the vestige of a puzzled frown creased the general's brow. 'I do not quite understand . . . but if what this cable — this demand, via our Hague Embassy — says is true, Yankovsky is being held . . . to ransom . . . for gold to the value of twenty million US dollars! . . . Am I correct in my assumption that if we accept and deposit gold to the value of twenty million US dollars in a certain numbered Swiss bank account, Yankovsky will be turned over to us alive? It sounds like a hoax, comrades — at our expense.'

'So I myself thought at first . . . now I

think not, comrade General. For example, these photographs our comrades mention in their cable identify Yankovsky beyond doubt . . . one in a very compromising situation. Yankovsky, in my opinion, has undoubtedly fallen into the hands of someone who is motivated primarily by mercenary reasons rather than — or as well as — political ones . . . '

'But those demands to Israel . . . ' interjected the general. ' . . . The threat to her secret atomic weapons plant at Dimona . . . The note she received from those people calling themselves the 'Friends for Peace' . . . We know the Israelis take that threat very seriously.'

'I believe that original threat was a genuine one. I have a theory, comrade General.'

'We need to work on *facts* not theories,' interrupted Kulik.

'Silence! comrade Colonel,' snapped the general. 'When we have heard what our comrade has to say, you can criticise — not before.'

Zigel saw a flush of red suffuse above his rival's collar. Kulik seemed to shrink visibly several inches in his seat.

'My theory is that someone — some organization? — is masterminding the Norwegian operation for these obscure terrorists whoever they are. I have examined the evidence so far from all angles . . . The modus operandi of the Palestinians is well enough known to us. After all, we in the KGB have been responsible for assisting in their fight against Zionism . . . '

'Quite, comrade Colonel,' interjected the general coldly, holding up his hand. 'We discussed that yesterday, if I recall.' The general was still embarrassed by the obvious facts which had been aired at length the day before: if Palestinian terrorists were responsible, they were now biting the hand that had once fed them.

'That is not, exactly, my point, comrade General.'

'I'm pleased to hear that. Go on . . . '

'My point is . . . if the Palestinians were responsible for this operation — which seems possible — they would need to be operational in Norway. In a country where

165

most people are light-complexioned, Arabs are anomalies — they stand out individually *and* in crowds. At some time they would need to show themselves. The Palestinians may have thought about this problem . . . My theory — my assumption — is that someone else is actually subcontracting the operation for them. Someone who is being paid with Arab money. However, my belief is that someone — an individual or organization, whatever it is — has no intention of letting the Palestinians use those Silent Men missiles of ours to blow Israel to kingdom come — perhaps trigger World War III . . . not when they see the possibilities of considerably extending the opportunity of increasing their fee several-fold . . . '

' . . . by putting a price on Yankovsky's head via the KGB?' interrupted the general, pleased with his own deductive powers.

'Exactly, comrade General, but even more than that.'

'*More*, comrade Colonel?'

'The other telegram I passed to you,

comrade General.'

'I did not quite understand the implications of that one. Please elucidate for me. Who is this American Hines with domestic problems our agent in Oslo cables us about?'

'Undoubtedly a CIA career agent, comrade General.'

'Oslo — Norway — must have several CIA career agents permanently working there. I fail to see the significance.'

'Permit me, comrade General,' and Zigel passed over a handwritten digest. 'This is an abstract I made after further studies of Yankovsky's file. It is self-explanatory, I think.'

The general scanned it and then, slowly, a comprehension dawned in his eyes.

'Good work, comrade. Now I see the point you are driving at. This man Hines has had much contact with Yankovsky in the past at the various scientific congresses they mutually attended. Yankovsky himself talks about him in his reports.' He paused and looked sideways towards Zigel. 'You're *sure* it's the same name.

Not a coincidence of names?'

'No, comrade General. I am *one hundred per cent* sure about that,' and Zigel looked towards Kulik and smiled.

'So you imply his presence in Norway at this moment has something to do with Yankovsky's defect . . . or rather Yankovsky's abduction — if *your* theory is correct . . . You think the CIA are mixed up with those who abducted Yankovsky?'

'Perhaps . . . very indirectly. My ideas on that might be a red herring to our present conversation so I will omit them. In this instance I believe it is very significant that Hines has suddenly turned up in Norway. It is only by that highly indiscreet telephone call he made to his wife in Washington over an open, public transatlantic line — which our agent in Oslo overheard — that we know he is in Norway now . . . He is one of the few CIA men who could be sure to recognize Yankovsky . . . '

'Then — as the British would say — we are involved in a 'Dutch auction'?' suggested the general, anxious to resolve the denouement of Zigel's theory, for now the penny had finally dropped for him — at least he hoped so. He also hoped his 'Dutch' pun was not lost on Zigel whom he recognized as a more literate, worldly person than himself. ' . . . Yankovsky's captors have offered the CIA the same bargain as they have offered us?'

'Exactly, comrade General.'

'This American agent,' began the general again pensively, ' . . . he appears to be upset about the domestic difficulty with his wife due to his hurried departure abroad . . . hence the foolishness of his breaking cover and talking directly to her in Washington over an open line . . . I congratulate you Colonel for putting 'two and two together' — as those wretched American detectives are fond of saying in that trashy Western literature I have to read as part of my duty to keep abreast with the progress of Western decadence . . . '

The general's subordinates round the table could barely suppress their mirth. It was common gossip in the corridors of Lubyanka that the general had a particular weakness for American and British detective and spy fiction. Zigel himself had recently seen his general reading a dog-eared copy of *From Russia with Love* and apparently enjoying it with gusto. He himself preferred the old Russian masters . . . Turgenev, Tolstoy, Gogol, Gorky . . . Yes, perhaps Gorky was his favourite — a real man of the people; an uncompromising realist who didn't conceal the seamy side of character. His own life in the KGB brought him cheek-by-jowl with the seamy side of life. Perhaps one day he would try to write a little in the vein of his old literary hero. Until then . . . The general was talking again, and Zigel snapped out of his brief reverie.

'Of course,' said the general, 'there is a further aspect which occurs to me in respect to this American . . . Hines.'

Zigel knew how to play on the general's vanity. The general, he'd long recognized, imagined himself as a shrewd, quick thinker — rather than a by-the-book hard-liner for which he owed his promotion to high office. Zigel sometimes made all the play towards the goal-mouth, then purposely faltered, passed and hung back to allow the general to kick the goal himself. He'd done so this time. It didn't pay to be over-bright *all* the time. He'd already made up a lot of the ground lost over the previous thirty-six hours. It seemed he was back in the general's favour. If the general himself hadn't actually said so, the expression now haunting Colonel Kulik's face, opposite, confirmed it.

'Further aspect, comrade General?'

'It occurs to me Hines is highly vulnerable — domestically. We could take advantage of his present vulnerability if, and when, we have to. We should always recognize that *dezinformatsiya* is not to be restricted to military and political matters . . . '

'Ah! I see your subtle point, comrade General. We could use his vulnerability to . . . divert him — if, or when, the need arises. Your thinking is ahead of mine, General. I fully understand now . . . '

'Good,' replied the general, his face momentarily breaking its standard grim expression to indicate self-satisfaction, 'then we shall now have open discussion round the table for additional ideas. Colonel Kulik, you may now have the floor if you so wish.'

Colonel Kulik had sufficient presence of mind to decline the invitation to follow in the wake of the star billing — there were no pickings left, only pitfalls. Demurely he passed to allow Major Sverchkov to catch the general's attention with some minor suggestions which should not be overlooked in any proposed setpiece ploy to apprehend Yankovsky.

The meeting finally broke up thirty minutes later. It had been agreed Colonel Zigel would fly to Oslo immediately to supervise the covert operation personally. Fortunately, he had no wife to pacify about his immediate, hurried departure abroad. He'd been divorced now for two years.

It was one of those coincidences in life that the KGB's code name for the new operation in Norway was 'Project Recovery'.

15

On the second day after departure from the Hook of Holland, and just after 1400 hours as indicated by the ship's clock, James Kerr disembarked at Kristiansand in south Norway.

Since leaving the Hook, on the trail of Peter Hasler, events had conspired to make his position on board the ferry untenable. He now judged it far too risky to remain where he was until the ferry docked in Oslo later that night. Sooner, rather than later, someone among the cabin staff, whom he'd been keeping at bay all morning by a subterfuge, was going to sniff out Kara Alstad's ripening corpse.

By remaining on board he would have had no chance to go to ground when the body was discovered. Ashore in Kristiansand he could catch a train for Oslo. The city would then swallow him up.

When Kerr walked off the ship at

Kristiansand, he used the landing-card made out for Peter Hasler.

Audaci favet fortuna.

It was a simple ploy. He realized the official at the bottom of the gangway collecting the cards would not require to see any passports. For convenience of passengers, the Norwegian immigration official travelling aboard the ferry had already inspected and stamped all passports shortly after passengers had come aboard at the Hook. Like Hasler he'd had his own passport stamped and received his Norwegian landing-card soon after leaving Holland . . . He'd found Hasler's card tucked inside the passport. By using Hasler's landing-card, instead of his own, he could put authority off his trail when they started a manhunt for the Englishman James Kerr — suspected murderer of Kara Alstad.

Once your cover as an agent is blown, you are no longer of use to the SOC. That message had got through to him as if he were one of Pavlov's famous dogs . . .

The ferry was scheduled to stop over in

Kristiansand approximately thirty minutes before sailing on to Oslo.

★ ★ ★

When George hadn't phoned him back from the ferry as he'd earlier promised, he grew apprehensive. Strange that George had failed to ring back his old pal Jake . . . Something *might* have gone wrong. George had told him that Alstad bitch was on board and now suspected she was shadowing him.

Someone snoopy like that could louse up the whole of their very covert op. Earlier, George had been more than a little worried that Solberg was a possible stool and had fouled things up for them, but Ranby and the other Norwegians had since called on Solberg's sister in Oslo and that part, Ranby said, he now had nicely under control.

Anyway, George had told him on the phone earlier to drive down to Kristiansand with Nilsen in the Merc to meet him there. George had broadly hinted on the phone he had immediate plans to dispose of that nosy-parker journalist. He'd also said there could be a guy travelling with her. George still wasn't altogether sure about that. Now there'd been no word from George for over ten hours, It wasn't like George. This morning Nilsen had phoned the ferry to get George paged. He'd tried three times, but the shipboard operator had told him no Peter Hasler had contacted the radio room. Anyway, he'd soon know why George was keeping a low profile after he and Nilsen met the ferry when she docked. George, he supposed, would have a lot to tell him when they met in Kristiansand.

★ ★ ★

Kara Alstad's body was found in the shower compartment twenty minutes after the ferry sailed for Oslo. Stewardess Olga Hansen screamed at the top of her voice when she saw the corpse. She needed assistance from her fellow stewardesses to get back to her quarters and then a generous double brandy before the Purser and Chief Steward could get a coherent word out of her.

Yes, the tall Englishman with the moustache had told her he was travelling on to Oslo. Earlier that morning he'd pressed a hundred-kroner note on her with instructions to delay the cleaning of his cabin until the ship had left Kristiansand. He'd told her he wished to catch up with some lost sleep. His request was by no means unusual with passengers going on to Oslo.

* * *

After Nilsen had checked with the immigration official, they now knew something was seriously wrong . . . They had patiently watched the gangway and looked at everyone who'd disembarked from the ferry. Then Nilsen had managed to get aboard. He'd checked the cabin booked in Peter Hasler's name and, except for his overnight luggage, found it empty. The stewardess he'd chatted up hadn't seen the occupant since the previous night. His bed hadn't been slept in either. There was definitely no George around — as incognito Peter Hasler or otherwise. Then how was it that George's landing-card was now lodged with the immigration people ashore? Nilsen had checked after drawing a blank on board — just in case they'd somehow missed George. There could only be one conclusion: Someone else had used it! To Nilsen's further enquiries, the official at the bottom of the gangway had told them he only vaguely remembered the man called Hasler. However, one thing he did recall was the man's elegant Zapata moustache. He also recalled seeing the same man walk in the direction of the railway station.

* * *

Captain Stig Berg was informed of events just after 1450 hours. Already the Purser had initiated a ship-to-shore contact with the Kristiansand Police. Ashore, the landing-cards handed in were in the process of being checked.

At 1504 hours, a black Volvo sedan, with POLITI written in bold white caps on its sides and an orange light flashing from its roof beacon, sped down Gyldenlöves gate and then turned into Vestre Strandgate and squealed to a stop outside a quayside office posted: Immigration Control.

When Inspector Arvid Lybeck and police driver Sergeant Nils Bakke entered the building, Alf Ryen, Chief Immigration Officer for the port, already had his answer. No one had landed at Kristiansand with the name James Kerr. He'd checked the cards three times since receiving the earlier telephone call from Police Headquarters. There could be no oversight.

Two minutes later a message was flashed back to Captain Stig Berg: *It is possible the passenger known as James Kerr is still aboard your ship. We need a full description.*

The information required came back fifteen minutes later.

'What do you say, Alf?' Asked Arvid Lybeck after they'd all digested stewardess Olga Hansen's description.

'Yes, indeed, there was such a man,'

confessed the chief immigration officer after only little thought. 'I recall him because somebody else enquired about him. The man you describe handed me a card in the name of Peter Hasler . . . Look, I have it here. I'm positive about that. The person who asked me earlier whether Hasler had landed was definitely a Norwegian. Big and brawny, probably a seaman or ex-military?'

Soon after, the Volvo with the two police officers, plus the bundle of landing-cards, sped back to Central Headquarters.

$$\star \quad \star \quad \star$$

He and Nilsen saw the man they'd been watching drink coffee in the station buffet walk out and into the toilet. Then he'd been wearing a moustache — no doubt at all about that. But he wasn't wearing it when he walked out again. There was only one conclusion to be drawn from the suspect's behaviour. This *was* the man who'd used George's landing-card.

Then Kovas and Nilsen had made their

plans. It was too public to make an intercept here. The guy was probably armed to the teeth — most likely with George's ironmongery for extras. He'd be watching his back carefully. Before the train pulled out, Nilsen did some quick phoning. When he put the phone down, he told him he'd arranged the rendez-vous and intercept further up the line. So now it was all set up . . . Nilsen would drive back the Merc while he took the train. He wanted to supervise this part of the intercept himself. He wanted no slip-ups. If George was gone — too bad. He had himself to think about from now on.

★   ★   ★

Back at Police Headquarters in Kristian-sand a group of assistants were assembled. Train timetables were con-sulted and several supernumeraries were delegated to telephone local hotels, boarding-houses, car-hire firms and taxi companies. Others divided the bundle of cards and began to assemble a list of names. When Arvid Lybeck knocked on the door of the superintendent's office a few minutes before 1700 hours to report progress, a manhunt was already under way in south Norway for the Englishman James Kerr.

* * *

The railway station at Kristiansand lies conveniently adjacent to the quayside. Passengers who wish to travel on by train can simply disembark from the ferry and walk the short distance across onto the station platform.

As soon as Kerr landed he consulted a railway timetable. As he'd anticipated, the Oslo-bound boat-train express left in fifteen minutes. After buying a second-class ticket, there was just time to eat a couple of cheese *smörbröd* and drink a cup of coffee in the station buffet. By now he was famished. He'd purposely missed breakfast aboard the ferry, preferring to remain in his cabin to prevent the stewardess entering to tidy his bed and clean the wash-room where overnight he'd parked Kara Alstad's ripening corpse.

When he'd eaten and finished his coffee, he ducked out into the toilet and emerged two minutes later minus his false Zapata and now wearing the passport face of Philip Gill. The Norwegian Police, he felt sure, would not be looking for the fugitive wanted by their colleagues in Holland.

The express left on time. It was due to arrive at Oslo's Vestbanest at 2210 hours. He settled down to watch the Norwegian countryside flash by and reflect on his circumstances.

He knew he'd be taking *some* risk boarding the Oslo boat-train express. When the alarm went out for the absent ferry passenger who'd occupied cabin 101 where Kara Alstad's body had been found, there'd bound to be a hue and cry . . . They might eventually deduce that the man who'd come ashore in Kristiansand as Peter Hasler was the very man to help them with their enquiries . . . They'd chance start looking for a man who'd removed his moustache. They'd tumble to the possibility that moustache was a false one to put them off the scent. It all depended on how quick the Norwegian Police were in circulating the rest of his description and how accurate that was. Once he reached Oslo and his safe house, the city would swallow him up.

He knew, however, he'd have been taking a bigger chance hanging around a small town like Kristiansand with a population of only a little over 30,000. When the balloon went up, the police would automatically check all hotels and *pensjonater*. Hailing a taxi and then driving out of town would also have provided a sure giveaway about his movements. Any driver would be sure to remember a tall Englishman and his destination.

It was not really surprising he'd had little sleep during the previous night. He'd remained puzzled by Kara Alstad's possible role. If she was an undercover agent of the Norwegian PO and had independently followed the American, as he suspected she'd done, the sooner he could report the facts and circumstances of events to the general, the sooner the general in turn could inform the appropriate Norwegian contact about it. He'd have to do it, of course, via the local hot-line direct to the general in Brussels as soon as he reached that safe house in Oslo. The general might not like it much when he heard he'd killed the American before their unit was ready to strike. Whatever, it was spilt milk and the main thing was to keep his cover intact until Oslo.

Aboard the boat-train, Kerr noticed the ticket-collector enter the open Pullman-style car. He inspected and then clipped his ticket and passed on without comment. Before reaching Oslo, stops were scheduled at Svenes, Gjerstad, Bo, Kongsberg and then Drammen. Oslo's Vestbanest would be the spot the police might choose for a reception committee if they had one in mind. There, at the line terminus, they could isolate and then surround the train and carefully check in turn every male passenger at the barrier. A classic set-piece intercept with less risk to other passengers. With this strong possibility in mind, he began to formulate a plan to leave the train earlier at Kongsberg or Drammen. He could finish his journey on to Oslo by bus.

There was still no outward sign of trouble after the train had passed Svenes and Gjerstad.

First signs of it came immediately after pulling out of Bo, just past the halfway mark to Oslo. That's when Kerr noticed an inquisitive character wandering slowly down the car from the direction of the engine.

The nondescript man looked suspicious and nosy. A Norwegian plain-clothes officer?

Maybe . . . but then he was possibly just overreacting. The result of a guilty conscience? The man could simply be someone looking to find a friend on the train. He certainly didn't *look* like a policeman.

As he approached, Kerr pretended to have his head buried in his copy of the *Aftenposten* he'd picked up at the station kiosk in Kristiansand. Squinting from under the paper, he noticed the man momentarily pause and give him an apparently casual once-over before he sauntered on. After he'd passed, Kerr could instinctively feel the man turning and then staring back to have another good look at him. The fact he was taller than the average man might select him for special scrutiny. It could be a factor that might draw attention to him in a manhunt.

He was tempted to turn round and meet the man's eyes. He resisted temptation for all of five minutes before he casually rose to his feet and wandered along the car to the toilet compartment located in the direction the inquisitive character had been heading when he passed him.

He spotted the man sitting at the end of the car. He was bent on playing the same cliché piece of theatre with his newspaper as he himself had done earlier.

As he passed, he noticed with a start the man was reading a copy of the *International Herald Tribune*.

Whoever he was, the anonymous man didn't seem to be in a hurry to make any contact. If he did represent trouble, he'd got himself positioned in the prime spot where he could cover any move of his quarry.

Inside the toilet compartment Kerr repositioned the Browning automatic in his waistband where he could snatch at it in a hurry if he needed it. Before leaving the compartment, he felt in his right-hand pocket to be reassured by the additional presence of the 'two-five Bauer sitting there. If things went wrong, he might need a back-up weapon.

He walked back to his old place halfway along the car, but at the last moment swiched to one of the empty seats opposite the direction he'd faced earlier so he could keep in his sights the man he now labelled 'Snoopy'. With his fingers he deftly made a small slit in the fold of his *Aftenposten* to use it as a surveillance opening. Then, from behind the raised newspaper, he watched.

He patiently watched Snoopy through the slit for over five minutes before he caught him looking down the car, his eyes raised just above the level of his *Herald*

Tribune. He caught him exercising the same manoeuvre several times during the next half hour or so.

Then, surprisingly, Snoopy suddenly folded his paper, rose to his feet and walked down the car towards him. He felt the adrenalin begin to pump and he instinctively slipped his hand inside his jacket where he could feel the security of the Browning's walnut butt. His hand felt moist.

Drawing abreast, Snoopy kept on walking without hesitation. When Kerr switched back to his original seat so as to look down along the car, the man had already passed out of view.

Kerr sat tight.

It was after the train pulled into Kongsberg he made the decision to stay put at least until Drammen . . . It was bigger than Kongsberg and only one hour's bus ride from Oslo. Potentially, if it came to it, there were more opportunities of giving Snoopy the slip in Drammen.

At Kongsberg quite a crowd boarded the train. For the first time since leaving Kristiansand the rail-car almost filled up. Two middle-aged matrons travelling together made a bee-line for the two empty places opposite him. They ignored him completely, and from their incessant chatter he soon deduced they were travelling to Oslo for a shopping trip and planned to stay overnight in the city.

The two matrons, locked in their own chatter, continued to ignore him. He concentrated on thinking out his future moves for the time when the train reached Drammen and he made a run for it. A few minutes out of Drammen he'd get up and visit the toilet again. When he came out of the toilet this time, he'd dodge back towards the rear of the train. A couple of cars farther along he'd stop to watch if Snoopy was still interested. If Snoopy followed towards the rear of the train . . . well, who could tell? At Drammen he'd have to take his chances. He couldn't afford to wait until they reached Oslo's Vestbanest where there could be a dozen or more well-armed snoopies lying in wait for him. If it came to it, he could explain . . . He didn't want to have to start any kind of explanation, even to the police . . . *Once your cover as an agent is blown, you are no longer of use to the SOC.*

Kerr noted that one of the matrons had opened a valise. On her knee she'd got *smörbröd* and two big flasks of coffee. For the first time since they'd boarded the train she acknowledged his stare. She smiled at him, he smiled back. The next thing he knew she'd pushed towards him a plastic cup filled with coffee. '*Vaer sa god*,' she said.

'*Takk. De er snill*,' he answered in his best Norwegian.

While he drank the coffee, the two matrons continued their excited chatter about their prospective shopping trip to the big city.

A few minutes later the one who'd given him coffee turned and smiled again. He felt obliged to say, '*Deres kaffe er deilig.*'

Actually, he didn't think it was very good coffee. It tasted stale and bitter; he was merely being polite telling her it was delicious. After the fortitudes of the past forty-eight hours he was feeling weary.

Coffee — even stale coffee — would help fortify his spirits. When the matron pressed another cupful on him, he didn't refuse. More coffee might help him overcome his lassitude. If he'd been reading Snoopy's attentions correctly, he'd need to be on his toes and fully alert when the train shortly pulled into Drammen.

Since the new influx of passengers at Kongsberg, the rail-car had grown unbearably stuffy and hot. His brow was wet with beads of sweat and his throat burned and ached. Aboard a British train he would have politely asked the two matrons if they'd mind if he opened the window to let in a little fresh air. Likely on a British train the windows would have been opened long ago — at the direct request of the female passengers. He'd travelled enough in Norway to know that such a request might be greeted by local matrons with looks of total disbelief. He knew these modern Vikings lived in horror of anything which had the slightest resemblance to a draught of cool air. Opening a window would likely result in

the matrons calling the conductor immediately. A conductor meant trouble.
There'd be a fuss. He couldn't afford to
be involved in any kind of contretemps
with authority. He remained impassive
— trying to ignore the stale, fetid air and
hoping that Drammen would soon appear
round the corner.

He even accepted a third cup of coffee
pressed on him. Then, out of the window,
at last he recognized the bare rocky
mountain that rises over Drammen. No
more than another five minutes at the
most and then, thank God, he'd be there!

He tried to gauge the exact moment to
get up and make his move down the car
towards the toilet.

By now he was feeling positively
nauseous; his head was swimming; his
eyes had difficulty maintaining focus. He
began to gasp for air.

He saw both matrons eyeing him curi-
ously. He started to say, '*Unnskyld* . . . '
and half staggered to his feet. He now
needed that toilet urgently to throw up.
But he didn't even start to get anywhere
near it or finish his excuses. The matron

who'd offered him coffee was pointing at his breast a small automatic pistol disguised under a white napkin. In broken English, and with menace in her words, she said, 'Just sit down again, Mr Kerr, or I will not hesitate to shoot you.'

Two seconds later he passed out.

16

When the boat-train from Kristiansand ground to a halt in Oslo's Vestbanest terminus dead on schedule, there was a reception committee numbering eleven officers assembled to intercept the Englishman James Kerr, wanted for questioning. In charge of operations was Inspector Jan Presterud of E-Gruppa[1] — Norway's élite, serious-crime squad.

The alert for James Kerr had come through several hours earlier on the hot-line from Kristiansand. At the time it came through, Jan Presterud, a man in his early forties, of classic Nordic looks and unrelenting blue eyes, had been sitting in his large, drab office inside the institutional greyness of E-Gruppa's headquarters in Oslo's Victoria Terrasse routinely checking reports.

Some said it was no accident that the

---

[1] Full title: *Etterforskningsgruppa*

authorities had seen fit to place E-Gruppa's headquarters in the same grey-grim building which forty years before had served as the headquarters of the dreaded Gestapo during Norway's darkest days. Those who said this had reasons to fear E-Gruppa's tough-minded officers.

Perhaps the most tough-minded of all the élite incumbents was Inspector Jan Presterud. More than once he'd been called a Fascist pig during the course of interrogating criminals he and his team had tracked down. Not that Norway was a country ridden with serious crime. Compared with some other Western European countries, Norway was almost a citizen's paradise. But since the sixties, murder, violence and armed robbery had gradually increased, as elsewhere. Every year now there were some forty or fifty murders to solve in Norway. E-Gruppa's officers could be proud of their record because, like the Mounties, they invariably got their man — and usually their woman too, since women nowadays were often involved in serious crime.

Certainly Jan Presterud wasn't going to let the Englishman slip through his net that easily. That's why, when he prepared his trap at Vestbanest and found the quarry had escaped, he wanted to know why his apparently foolproof plan to apprehend the man known as James Kerr had failed.

'The Englishman must have skipped the train at Kongsberg or Drammen,' suggested Sergeant Roar Overn, Presterud's chief assistant.

'What does Svein Moen have to say about it?' asked Presterud with a touch of cynicism in his voice. 'He was detailed, so you told me, to tail any suspect from Bo and then keep a low profile. Remember?'

'That's the trouble at the moment,' answered Overn. 'He hasn't reported in yet. He could still be tailing him, some place. I told you Ole Rusten saw Moen get on the train, and we know he spotted a suspect because of that confirmatory message he passed back from Kongsberg.'

'So you're convinced he's still tailing that suspect?' Presterud arched an eyebrow to underscore his disbelief.

'Tell you the truth, chief, no, I don't. I think something went wrong on the train. I've got a team of locals checking both at Kongsberg and Drammen.'

Ten minutes later Overn brought his chief up to date. 'A total blank at Kongsberg, but the local boys say they've now questioned the stationmaster in Drammen. He says he vaguely recalls seeing a man of Moen's description get off the train. But after that the boys think he's a little confused because he says if it was him, he was apparently following a male and two females who looked like housewives. These people, he says, were supporting another male — a friend? — who'd fainted in the train. The stationmaster says *he thinks* the same man as he vaguely identifies as Moen then got in the same vehicle as the others and they all drove off. Maybe a black Merc, but he can't be sure of that either. His excuse is he was very busy after the train came in. All in all it sounds like a bum lead ... There could have been several people on that train looking like Moen, and our friend the stationmaster spotted the wrong one. I mean, Kerr's known to be travelling solo. Anyway, I expect Moen will be ringing in soon to report . . . '

When the trussed-up, very dead corpse of Sergeant Svein Moen — with a 9mm slug fastened to the base of his skull — was finally found at 6 a.m. the following morning on the outskirts of Drammen by a two-man crew of a local police Volvo, V for Victor, Presterud, who through the long night had feared the worst, knew he was dealing with an extremely ruthless killer.

In the meantime the investigative wheels had been turning. At midnight, when the ferry from the Hook finally docked at Piperviken, Presterud and his team of E-Gruppa experts had gone aboard immediately. At the orders of the Kristiansand Police, the cabin containing Kara Alstad's corpse had been locked and guarded until the ferry reached Oslo. In two hours the forensic experts had finished their work, and the body removed ashore. To Captain Stig Berg's relief, the ship was released to sail on schedule the following morning on the understanding the murder cabin would be sealed until they returned to Norway in case E-Gruppa's officers wished to inspect it again later.

The fingerprints found in the murder cabin and those found in Kara Alstad's cabin were circulated immediately to Scotland Yard and Interpol; and because the ferry had sailed from Holland, to the Dutch Police. They were tagged: 'Urgent, very prompt action, please.'

Another message, concerning another query, was flashed to the FBI in Washington DC.

A reply message from the Dutch Police was on Inspector Presterud's desk just a few minutes after the local report came in about the finding of Svein Moen's body in Drammen.

'Thank God we live in a computer age!' Presterud remarked to Overn across the room as he digested the hot-line report from Holland. Neither had slept a wink all night.

'We've scored then?' queried Overn who was given to using idiomatic speech as most of E-Gruppa's officers were wont to do.

'Yes. I'll say we have!' confirmed Presterud. 'However, it says here they don't belong to any of the James Kerrs the Dutchies have on their computerized records . . . but some prints from both cabins check out very positively with a very hot number. Guess who? — one Philip Gill.'

Presterud and Overn already knew about Gill. The Dutch Police had contacted the Oslo Police, routinely, a day back to glean more information about a Norwegian national called Backer who'd been found murdered in a hotel in the Hague. They'd told E-Gruppa the hotel room had been occupied earlier by an Englishman called Philip Gill . . . They'd also noted the report of the mysterious killing of Backer — apparently by an Englishman — in foreign language newspapers they'd scanned the day before. It was common practice for all E-Gruppa's officers to read the influential foreign press to keep abreast of serious crime in other countries. The British

Daily Telegraph and the *International Herald Tribune* were English-language newspapers much favoured by E-Gruppa's officers. Sergeant Svein Moen was one of those who'd favoured reading the latter.

Just before seven, the phone on Presterud's desk jangled. It was his immediate chief, the *förstebetjent* — equivalent to a US captain of detectives or a British chief inspector. He'd just risen from his bed. To his enquiries, Presterud told him about the discovery of Moen's body and the message from Holland. To another query he replied, 'You mean that missing American passenger — Peter Hasler? . . . No, he hasn't shown up anywhere. Looks as if our earlier theory is the right one. Kerr — Gill — must have robed and murdered him, then tossed him overboard. It appears that one of the barmen on the ferry was the last to see Hasler alive. When we interviewed the crew earlier this morning, this man says he thinks someone answering the description of Kerr was sitting next to Hasler in the bar. We know, too, that someone had been trying to phone Hasler from Norway. Three calls were logged, but they couldn't locate him. The stewardess says she's certain Hasler didn't sleep in his cabin. The clincher to that murder theory is that unclaimed left luggage in Hasler's cabin. I'm querying the FBI in Washington. Of course, no reply yet. Incidentally, the lab boys found fresh sperm in Kara Alstad. Looks like Kerr — Gill — raped her before strangling her.'

After the chief inspector rang off, Presterud sat pensively at his desk. Another query gestated in his mind. 'How many autos were nicked in Drammen yesterday?' he suddenly asked Overn across the room.

'Wait, chief. I'll check.' Overn picked up his own phone.

A couple of minutes later he had the answer. 'None, chief. It was a clean night.'

'You're sure? I want to be *absolutely* certain about this. Tell them to give me the Drammen nick. I'll talk to their desk myself.'

Overn had his connection transferred to the other phone. Then the inspector satisfied himself the information passed on to Overn had been correct. The desk sergeant of the local police insisted no vehicles of any kind had been stolen — none at least reported as stolen. In fact there hadn't been a vehicle theft reported in Drammen for the past three days.

Presterud sat back again in his swivel chair; he raised his feet and rested them on his desk top and folded his arms. To Overn he looked a million miles away, locked in thought.

'What is it, chief?' he enquired cautiously. Presterud could sometimes be tetchy if his train of thought was interrupted.

'We have a real problem with this one, Roar.'

Overn's eyes blinked. The inspector didn't often call him by his first name. Not in the office anyway. He reserved that for those occasions when they let their hair down — usually when they'd successfully cracked a tough case and drank a Pils together to celebrate. On such occasions Overn even called his chief Jan. But not today. Not in the office.

Overn replied, 'Problem? I see no problem, chief — except there might be a shoot-out with that English son-of-a-bitch, and we've got to find and stop him before he kills again. We think he's some kind of trained killer. He's gone rogue for some reason — probably blown a valve. Remember it happened before with those GIs who fought in Vietnam. Those ex-Russells' Rangers who couldn't settle down and who turned bank robber. When an animal goes rogue, there's only one solution,' and he drew the front edge of his right hand across his throat in an unambiguous gesture.

Presterud, who'd only been listening with half an ear, suddenly swung his legs off the desk, unfolded his arms and sat upright in his chair. 'You've missed the point, my lad. Look, just think about it. If no autos or other vehicles were nicked in Drammen, how the hell did Kerr manage to get Moen shifted three kilometres down the road? Remember, our late colleague was a heavy-weight. Carry him bodily through Drammen? I don't think so. Load him on a motorcycle, bicycle, handcart, horse? Not a chance! He was found on an area of muddy ground yet his shoes were not caked in mud. He was trussed up and killed elsewhere. Kerr would have needed transport, and why would he bother to drop Moen three kilometres out of Drammen? Someone, working solo on the run, doesn't work like that. There *was* a vehicle involved, and we know he didn't use a taxi. I think that clue the stationmaster passed on wasn't a bum one after all. Otherwise nothing adds up ... And you're forgetting what the stewardess and radio operator aboard the ferry told us ... and what that immigration officer passed on from Kristiansand. *Someone* had been asking for Hasler; and according to the immigration laddie, the same party seemed a lot interested in the description of the character who'd used Hasler's landing-card. Then, why? — have you asked yourself ... why would Kerr murder a Norwegian in a hotel room in the Hague and then come running to Norway and leave a trail of carnage in his wake? ...'

The phone on Presterud's desk jangled again to interrupt him. As Overn listened, he noticed his chief's eyes change focus and harden at the impact of some news. He heard him answer, 'Okay, sir, but I don't like it. In a case like this we need the public's and the media's co-operation for leads,' and then he slammed down the receiver.

'Would you believe it,' said Presterud, redirecting his attention to Overn, 'the PO boys have been in touch with the Old Man. He says they've insisted we keep our enquiries re Kara Alstad's killing and Hasler's disappearance at strictly low-profile level. Whatever, they want the press kept out of it.'

'Secret service stuff, then. Wow!' exclaimed Overn. 'Mamma mia! I hope it's not those Jews and Arabs at it again. Kerr's not a Jew or an Arab, is he?'

Overn's remarks were apropos the events some years back when a group of hit-men from Israel's Mossad descended on Norway to hunt down a group of Palestinians believed to be living in Lillehammer, a small town 80 miles north of Oslo. To compound the offence in E-Gruppa's eyes, the Mossad had assassinated the wrong Arab. E-Gruppa's officers had won praise from the Norwegian press from cracking the case quickly, but at the same time they'd caused a great deal of embarrassment inside Norway's Secret Service and their diplomatic corps who'd turned a blind eye to the Mossad presence in Norway because they were known to be hunting the Munich Olympic assassins.

Unknown to Inspector Jan Presterud, Roar Overn and the fugitive James Kerr, events had conspired to make the Lillehammer affair small beer indeed compared with the new crisis that threatened.

17

At their secret headquarters on the outskirts of Tel Aviv, the Mossad already knew about the murder of Kara Alstad before Jan Presterud and his E-Gruppa team boarded the North Sea ferry when she docked in Oslo.

Their agent, Kara Alstad (code-named Hannah) — offspring of Jewish refugee grandmother Sarah Bernstein — had already got a message through that a man suspected of being James Kerr was on his way back to Norway. The man in Oslo who'd received it from aboard the ferry, and then given Hannah some information from the files in return, was Anders Tovalsen (code-named Felix) — a 'control' Mossad agent also of Jewish descent and now employed undercover as a Scandinavian import agent. One of his speciality lines was Israeli citrus fruits.

Tovalsen had been in his rented flat in Oslo's fashionable Incognito gate — his address was a good Jewish joke, he'd always thought — when his phone jangled and the news came through. The female voice said, 'Glad I caught you, Felix. I haven't much time. I've just slipped out and I'm phoning from a private number. There's a hell of a panic on at HQ. Hannah's dead! — murdered, I think. When I've got more news, I'll ring you back.'

A lot of matzo had been eaten and many lessons learnt since the days of the Lillehammer debacle back in '73 when Mossad agents got the wrong man. The operation had subsequently invoked much adverse publicity in the world's press about Israel's Secret-Service methods. The Mossad's Lillehammer hit-group had been mostly recruited from amateurs who were badly trained and badly informed. Since Lillehammer, E-Gruppa's HQ in Victoria Terrasse had been penetrated by a highly trained and motivated Mossad agent, admittedly she was not a policeman herself — that would have been too much to aim for — but a communications clerk with access to messages in and out of the building was probably the next best thing. In many ways she'd proved to be a lot more useful than a policeman. As a by-product, a lot of significant economic intelligence had filtered back to Tel Aviv in the two years since Ida Plevsky (code-named Debra) — a highly intelligent refugee Jewess of Polish descent, now a naturalized Norwegian with a degree in economics — had managed to land herself a job with E-Gruppa. No one could possibly have foreseen what a key role Ida Plevsky was to play in the future international crisis that loomed ahead for Israel.

The Mossad also had an internal score to settle with its own Shin Beth departmental arch-rival the Agab Modi'in (Military Intelligence) who in the past had been jealous of the Mossad's successes. The blunders in Lillehammer — and then a month later when the Mossad was involved in an illegal hijacking of a civilian airliner over Lebanese airspace because it was believed to contain George Habash, the leader of the terrorist group PFLP — were the kind of ammunition the Agab Modi'in and its backers in the Knesset had been waiting for in order to discredit the Mossad. Had the Mossad shot the right man in Lillehammer; had George Habash been apprehended aboard the hijacked airliner, it would have been a different story. The Agab Modi'in hadn't in fact stopped crowing about their rival's deficiencies until they themselves, caught out by their own head-in-the-sand blunders, had almost lost Israel the Yom Kippur War. Inside Israel's Secret Service (the Shin Beth), rivalry between the Mossad and the Agab Modi'in had festered to almost open warfare level. Only the intervention of the politicians kept the two factions from each others' throats. In such an atmosphere there was practically no interchange of information about respective activities between these two departments of the Shin Beth.

Anders Tovalsen was one of the few men in Norway that day who did not *immediately* suspect James Kerr of being Kara Alstad's murderer. The worst had probably happened! There'd always been a risk in Hannah shadowing CIA-turncoat Peter Hasler. The man was a known ruthless killer who'd never hesitated to protect his own skin. Solberg had been murdered, now Hannah . . .

Tovalsen never visited the Israeli Embassy. To openly call at the embassy might compromise his cover. Curious eyes watched the comings and goings of every embassy in Oslo. He rendezvoused with Uri Cohen — newly arrived back hotfoot from Tel Aviv — in the open-air cafe near the Studenterlund in busy Karl Johan gate.

He told Cohen the bad news.

'The bastard!' Cohen drew his hand across his face. 'Then Brand must have discovered she was shadowing him. He may even have suspected she'd got wind of his scheme to double-cross his friends and deliver the Russian into the hands of the highest bidder . . . the first to meet his terms. Only Brand could have made that offer to our embassy in the Hague. He would never have risked negotiating a deal like that from Oslo.'

'Exactly as I read it too,' answered

Tovalsen. 'And we can assume he's offered the same deal to the Russians and the CIA — or why would he stipulate 'to the highest bidder'. What was it? 'Substantial bids over twenty million US dollars' — or rather its market equivalent in gold. I wonder if the Russians and the CIA will play ball?'

'Even if they do, they'd both be suspicious whether he could deliver. In spite of those convincing photographs, they'd want to view the real goods first before depositing the ante. Trouble is, Yankovksy would be coming cheap at that price if those 'Friends for Peace' aren't bluffing us . . . The Russians, for obvious reasons, would gladly pay it just to get him back. The CIA would love to get their hands on him for his inside technical know-how and the bonus of picking up those Soviet missiles for themselves — *if* they exist and we're not so sure they do. As for us . . . '

'But the prime minister says no deal?'

'Right. Our holier-than-thou policy of absolutely no deals with any kind of anti-Zionist terrorists remains inviolate

214

. . . Anyway, the prime minister himself doesn't believe any of this missile thing is true. He'd rather believe what his 'friend' the Soviet president told him. Those *zhlubs* in the Agab Modi'in are all of a like mind . . . Back in Tel Aviv the Memuneh is having a hard time persuading those boneheads that this *could* be the real thing. They say we've cried wolf too often. We've got to crack this one on our own, Anders . . . You, me and Debra versus those 'Friends for Peace', plus Brand and his friends . . . Incidentally, when the time comes, he's all mine . . .'

Tovalsen motioned with his hand to interrupt, but Cohen ignored it.

' . . . Meantime we're going into the dirty-tricks department ourselves. We're going to leak the news to the Palestinians or the 'Friends for Peace' whoever they are that Brand — Hasler — planned on double-crossing them. To put another spanner in the works, we'll leak the same story to the KGB and the CIA. That kind of story could set up a few waves and engender distrust, suspicion and possible mayhem all round. In the confusion we might be able to make a grab for Yankovsky ourselves . . . '

'Hold your horses, Uri,' cut in Tovalsen finally. 'One little snag. Hasler's missing apparently. For my money it sounds like he's dead. Debra phoned again just before I came out to meet you. According to her, a landing-card made out for Hasler has been handed in at Kristiansand, but E-Gruppa now believe the man who handed in the card was James Kerr masquerading as Hasler.'

'You mean Kerr's knocked him off?'

'Looks that way, at least to me it does. According to Debra, E-Gruppa have questioned the crew of the ferry over the phone. Brand's — Hasler's — luggage is still in his cabin. There was a muster of passengers and a head-count. The ferry was searched end to end. The cabin stewardess told the police Hasler's bed hadn't been slept in. There could be no way he could get off before the ferry reached Kristiansand — except the obvious one that springs to mind.'

'Overboard, you mean? You think Kerr's killed him and dumped him overboard? Holy mother of Moses! Then Kerr's balls'd up Brand's plans for sure. Maybe he's balls'd up our own plans too, Anders . . . Except . . . let's think about it . . . now with Brand out of the way, no one else is going to get a chance of taking delivery of Yankovsky . . . He is all ours now. No one else knows where he is but we might if that Dramsfjord phone number Debra passed on checks out. We're still not sure where Kerr fits into the jigsaw. He's a rogue piece, but he's actually done us a big favour . . . Whoever he is, maybe he's just put himself in line for the Star of David for services rendered . . . '

18

On landing in Oslo, Hines was met and immediately chaperoned to a waiting Volvo by Lt Morgan Lucas (the third) USN Intelligence (Scandinavian Ops) and Reidar Eriksen — introduced by Lucas as a senior agent in the Norwegian PO Secret Service.

Lucas had news for Hines: 'Plans are changed. You can read through the decoded cables later . . . but the gist of things is that Yankovsky's been offered to us for a premium by a third party . . . '

'You mean,' cut in Hines, 'Yankovsky's been kidnapped? He's being ransomed?'

'Something like that. Anyway, your people and mine have sent word back from Washington they'll play ball. Your boss Holmes is due to fly over and help conduct negotiations. Problem at the moment is they're not absolutely sure whether this party who says he's got Yankovsky can or will actually deliver. He made his initial offer through the CIA man at the Hague Embassy — complete with some very convincing art work. He said he'd be in touch again next time through the embassy in Oslo, but so far our boys there haven't heard another whisper. So it might be a try-on . . . Might even be some kind of a ploy by the KGB to louse up our own chances — or find out how much we know. Whatever, we are supposed to await further orders — unless, that is, our Norwegian friends find out where Yankovsky is being held. If that's the case, we go in and collect him without paying the premium.'

'Hold it a minute, Lucas,' cut in Hines again. 'Let me take this in. Who do we think is offering us Yankovsky?'

'Top of the short-list is one of your ex-CIA colleagues — a guy called George Brand from Clandestine Services Directorate who went AWOL a year back and turned freelance. Now masquerading as Peter Hasler, he's suddenly gone missing off a North Sea ferry. Another of your colleagues, someone called Jake Kovas, is also now AWOL and no one knows where he is. It seems that Brand and Kovas were one-time dirty-tricks buddies and someone's put two and two together . . . The fact that some secret NATO spy outfit has reported Peter Hasler dodging mysteriously between Hamburg, the Hague and Norway, and the man who contacted the CIA man at the embassy in Holland seems to have known the right modus operandi for a covert contact, makes the brass almost sure he's mixed up with this Yankovsky business.'

In the Volvo driving into Oslo, Hines — alone on the back seat — couldn't help but compare the contrasting styles of his two companions in mufti up front. Lucas, aged about twenty-sixish, was dark, short and wiry, dapper, olive-complexioned, smooth-skinned; an obvious Bostonian in speech and breeding — the kind who could opt for an easy ride in the navy as an admiral's social aide-de-camp had he so wished.

By contrast, Eriksen, who had the wheel, was what the Ivy Leaguers would refer to as a 'rough diamond'. He was somewhere around the middle thirties, blue-eyed and fair-skinned — a Scandinavian giant of a man. Dapper was not a word one could ever have used about Eriksen in any context. He might just have stepped off the bridge of an Antarctic whaler; he wore a dark, greasy duffle jacket, and his face bore what seemed like a three-day-old bleached stubble. He didn't look like any kind of career secret service man and this, Hines guessed, was exactly the impression Eriksen was hoping to give to the world at large.

'Reidar's got you a room fixed up at his place,' explained Lucas as they drove along. 'We don't want you showing your face in a hotel or at the embassy. There are too many curious and prying eyes in Norway just now. Holmes will bunk somewhere else when he arrives.'

'Any actual signs or news of Yankovsky?' asked Hines.

'No actual sightings yet,' answered Eriksen, 'but we've a shrewd idea of the districts where he could be holed up if those missiles *are* in the Oslofjord . . . I'll brief you when we get back to the house and then we can look at the maps and charts . . . '

Hines had already noted at the airport that Eriksen spoke a familiar and fluent brand of English. Not the Old Bostonian clipped speech of Lucas — more a New York vernacular modified out of Wisconsin.

' . . . Trouble is,' added Eriksen, 'I'm sure we've got strong competition from the Mossad as well as the KGB.'

'You mean they've both already got people here in Norway looking for Yankovsky?' asked Hines.

'The Mossad, for sure — and who can blame them if that rumour someone plans to blow up Dimona *is* kosher. It's a foregone conclusion the Russians will be after Yankovsky themselves. However, the Mossad might know even more about him than we or the Ivans. We've got a twenty-four-hour tail on one of the known Mossad agents who's been very active here over the past day or two. And who knows? He or some of his contacts might lead us straight to Yankovsky. Then *we* can move in like Lucas here just said. We can also be sure the KGB won't be very far behind. It's a question who reaches Yankovsky first . . . The Ivans might just have some contingency plan to knock him off — that's if they can't see a way of picking him up cleanly for delivery to Lubyanka.'

'So his secrets — if not already betrayed to others — die with him?'

'Something like that, but for my money I expect they would make an effort to get him home in one piece — so at least he could assist in picking up all that expensive and embarrassing hardware he was careless enough to help drop in the Oslofjord just a while back. If that little lot doesn't get picked up by you *or* the Ivans, *my* government's going to be a little hysterical when we have to tell them the bad news . . . In the PO we don't like to panic our democratically elected members unless we have to.'

'You definitely want them moved then . . . by us *or* the Russians?'

'That's the general idea . . . But don't you boys get the wrong idea, we'd rather

Uncle Sam get first refusal; that's why we've agreed to pitch in with you, covertly . . . We really don't fancy doing a duo act with the Ivans — not unless we have to. So long as you boys can clear up that highly lethal backyard rubbish without any mess or noise, we play cool with the Ivans.'

'If we decide they're too hot to handle?' asked Hines. 'Remember, the Russians have leaked the news they're supposed to be booby-trapped by Yankovsky and the man himself has lost his marbles.'

Eriksen, eyes fixed on the road ahead, shrugged his shoulders. 'Then in the end we might have no option. Don't you boys forget we and the Ivans share the same backyard up north. We try to be neighbourly. They might come out in the open and ask us to act like honest neighbours and help recover something that fell over the fence by mistake from their side. Our politicians are so shit-scared of the Ivans they would tell us to co-operate in a neighbourly fashion.'

Hines was taken aback by the apparent attitude of the Norwegian PO. He was about to argue the point, but Lucas, who had already turned his head and was looking back at him, signalled with his eyes not to pursue this particular line with Eriksen. It was now clear to Hines it was an uneasy liaison that the CIA and US Naval Intelligence had established with the Norwegian PO. They were prepared to co-operate but only so far.

Hines and Lucas remained silent; Eriksen, however, indicated he wished to talk more on the subject. ' . . . What we don't know, of course, is whether the Israelis might try to get in on those missiles before you or the Ivans. We'd prefer to keep them right out of it.'

Lucas was facing forwards again. Hines was still curious. 'How would that be possible? We know they don't have any subs capable of picking up objects as large as medium-range ballistic missiles . . . '

'But the French have!' chipped in Eriksen. 'Maybe the South Africans, too, for that matter. Our mutual NATO ally, in particular, is a pretty dark horse. They're very pally with the Israelis at the moment. Don't forget it was the French who helped the Israelis set up the Dimona atomic plant complex in the first place. There's an on-going secret inter-change of nuclear technology between the Frenchies and the Israelis that you boys in Washington know all about. In turn the Israelis are also pretty thick with the South Africans. They've a lot in common. Remember, they're both outsiders on the international scene. In a jam, people like that stick together.'

'Do you think the French SDECE know about the threat to Israel?' asked Hines.

'Not from us they don't — or from your boys either, I guess; but I suspect the Agab Modi'in have filled them in, even if their buddies in the Mossad haven't. We've already assumed they have.'

'So it could develop into a messy three- or four-runner contest to be first to grab Yankovsky *and* his ironmongery,' said Hines, expressing his thoughts out loud. 'It might get a little crowded in the Oslofjord.'

'You bet!' agreed Eriksen.

19

When James Kerr recovered conscious-
ness, he noticed all around him was
pitch-black. First noise he heard was the
gentle lapping of water — the characteristic lapping of water on the strakes of a
clinker-built boat?

Then he discovered he couldn't move
his hands very far; and when he tried to
reach out, he realized he was manacled.
His legs were free but like jelly. His head
punched out a rhythm that wasn't a bad
imitation of Thor's hammer pounding
away inside his skull. His throat felt
parched and wretched.

Then he remembered the drugged
coffee and the two middle-aged matrons
in the train . . . nausea . . . and then
sinking into unconsciousness.

He realized he was lying on some kind
of mattress — a cold and slightly damp
mattress. The distinct pungent whiff of
stale fish and bilge-water pervaded the

air. He got little satisfaction from concluding he was imprisoned aboard — and low down — in some kind of small vessel. A commercial fishing-vessel?

He lay in a half dream-like torpor for what he judged was a little more than an hour. Not a chink of light penetrated the black-box prison. One thing was certain, the vessel was rock steady. He reasoned it couldn't be anchored in any open seaway — the open seaway of the Oslofjord for example. Maybe the boat was anchored by a wharf or in a quiet backwater neck of the Oslofjord? Somewhere like the Dramsfjord perhaps? Except in something approaching gale-force winds, a small fishing-vessel lying at anchor in the Dramsfjord wouldn't pull at her chains.

He heard the noise of a movement outside, then the rattle of the cabin door lock when it was opened.

A chink of light suddenly cascaded to a flood force. When his eyes adjusted, the face he saw wasn't Snoopy's, but it wasn't that of a total stranger either. He couldn't place it at first. Then he recalled it was a face that had registered in the train. A face that had been aboard from Kristian-sand and had apparently been quietly minding its own business just a couple of seats back from him. It wasn't minding its own business now.

'Up on your feet, and no smart-ass tricks!' The accent and vernacular was American, New York East Side or New Jersey? The man backed up his command with the wave of an automatic that looked familiar. It was. Kerr now recognized it was probably the same Browning pistol he'd been wearing in his waistband when he'd keeled over in the train.

With the gun pressed hard in his back, he was directed up a companion way into some kind of saloon. He noted the only daylight illumination came from a large, glazed skylight. He couldn't see out.

Now he was absolutely certain he was aboard a fishing-vessel. An ex-fishing-vessel from the looks of things. It was probably around eighty, eighty-five feet long. It was wide-beamed. It was a distinct — now outdated — design familiar to him from his own north-east background. She'd probably been built a quarter of a century back to work as a combination purse-seiner and long-liner. From appearances in the saloon, she'd been crudely modified to be used as a houseboat. Nowadays it wasn't likely a vessel in her condition ever put to sea for serious fishing work.

Using the Browning automatic as a pointer, the man indicated he should seat himself in a low upholstered chair, positioned in one corner. He didn't argue. Physically, he felt in no shape to argue.

The man was green-eyed, hawk-faced, yellow-skinned, and wore standard, non-descript landlubber clothes. With a complexion like that, Kerr knew he wasn't dealing with any kind of full-time pro sailor.

'How about a drink of water?' asked Kerr. 'My throat's on fire. Those two matrons back in the train almost overdid their Arsenic-and-Old-Lace act.'

The man's face remained impassive, but he reached out towards the cut-glass flask Kerr had spotted on the saloon table. The man poured some water into a matching glass tumbler. The flask and tumblers sitting unsupported on the table seemed to confirm Kerr's theory the fishing-boat wasn't going any place where the water got choppy. Not immediately anyway.

Kerr reached out with his manacled wrists and grasped the glass two-handed. He drank the contents greedily. 'How about a refill?' he asked.

'Maybe later when you've said your piece,' the man answered belligerently.

'What about?'

'You'll find out soon enough.'

At that moment the door leading down from the wheelhouse opened. A rough, mean-looking character, garbed like a professional salt, clambered down the companion way. He was wearing a heavy, double-knit Norwegian *genser*, blue denims and a dark, peaked cap without a badge. His face *was* windburnt; his eyes a washed-out blue. Kerr knew that on dry land he'd walk with a sailors' roll to match the rest of him. He was obviously the sea-going half of the partnership. He recognized him as Arne Ranby. He was one of those neo-Nazi business colleagues of Hasler's he and Olaf had been keeping their eyes on. Agewise he placed the American around the same age as Ranby — the late thirties.

The two men didn't exchange any kind of greetings. The play had been devised; the players cast. Hostility seeped across the saloon towards him like a poison gas.

Ranby, addressing him in a neutral tone, said, 'How did you get hold of the Browning and those papers?' Kerr noted Ranby's marked American-English accent.

'I found them lying on a boat-deck,' Kerr answered.

Kerr didn't see more than the flash of the movement as the man from the train reached out with the flat of his hand and caught him square across the cheek-bone. The taste of bile rose in his throat, and he fought to hold down the water he'd just drunk.

'That's just a starter,' said the man from the train. 'Any more smart-assed answers and I'll show you some more tricks in my repertoire.'

'Hold it a minute, Kovas,' said Ranby. 'We don't want Mr Kerr going to sleep on us again — not just yet anyway. Remember, he's got some important questions to answer first.'

' . . . So you picked up that Browning off the deck,' echoed the one he now knew as Kovas. 'Same place, I suppose, you just happened to come by that landing-card you handed in? Same place you found that green passport you were carrying? Same place you came by those pictures and that wallet and billfold with the name-tag — Peter Hasler?'

His head was bent low and pressed close to Kerr's, waiting for an answer. 'That's right,' Kerr replied and then gritted his teeth to wait for the hand to lash out again.

It didn't.

Instead Kovas pressed his face closer. 'So you think you're a tough cookie. Let's see how tough you really are. I'm going to work him over, Ranby.'

'Not yet, Kovas,' said Ranby. Then it was the Norwegian's turn to press his face closer. 'Kovas is the violent one. I prefer more subtle approaches. If you don't come up with the answers, Kovas is bound to insist we try his methods. Hasler was his buddy. Remember that. Now, let's not waste any more time. We have assumed that somehow you have disposed of Hasler. How, we do not know. We shall not waste time finding out. We presume he is dead. However, we should like to know *exactly* why you came to Norway and why you killed him. If you tell us and we accept your explanation, you can later go free. If you do not tell us — or we find your explanation . . . unacceptable, then I'm afraid we shall have to make other plans for you.'

'What guarantees have I you'll keep your word?'

'None, Mr Kerr. Absolutely none, but then you are in no position to bargain, are you?'

'Then you'll kill me anyway.' His own words struck chill in his bones. 'So why should I bother telling you anything?'

'To spare yourself unnecessary pain . . . Perhaps we may kill you . . . perhaps not. You are like a condemned man in the death cell awaiting the promise of a possible pardon. I have just given you a glimmer of hope, but only a glimmer. We might even keep you alive as a . . . hostage. Have you ever studied the subtleties of interrogation, Mr Kerr? Those who have studied the behaviour of the caged human animal facing possible death — or torture — agree unanimously that in desperation it will clutch at any straw to save its miserable skin . . . I give you a choice: me or Kovas. However, I must warn you, if I do not like your answer — or if I do not get an answer — I will let Kovas try his more unconventional methods of extracting the truth from you. I believe Kovas has had excellent training and experience in this field. If he too fails, you will not be aware of how we dispose of your earthly remains. That I promise you. Have I made your position clear?'

'Crystal-clear,' Kerr answered.

'Right, then please begin . . . '

Escape had been the only thought dominating Kerr's mind since Kovas had brought him up to the saloon. But how was he going to escape if he let them interrogate him still manacled with handcuffs? Somehow he'd have to get them to remove the cuffs — if only for a couple of minutes. Delaying tactics of some kind seemed his only hope.

Kerr said, 'All right, Ranby, I'm a realist. I'd sooner skip any of Kovas' Chinese torture treatment. However, before I talk, I'd like to feel comfortable. I need to make one of those very pressing, very personal calls of nature. I wouldn't want to mess up your saloon here halfway through saying my piece . . . After I've visited the can, I'll tell you anything you want to know . . . It's Solberg you want to know about too, isn't it?'

Kerr saw both interest and suspicion gestate — first in Ranby's eyes and then in his face. 'Very well, you have whetted my appetite, but if this is just an attempt to stall or escape, I promise you it will be the very last time you drop your pants.'

Turning to Kovas, he added, 'I suggest you take him to the heads for'ard and watch the bastard like a hawk. If he makes trouble, kill him.'

'It would be a pleasure!' Kovas replied, almost drooling at the prospect. Kerr knew then he was faced with a duo of fanatics.

At the end of the passageway they reached a door. Kovas, waving the Browning, motioned him to stand to one side. Then the American kicked open the door. 'Right,' he said. 'Inside and do your stuff.'

Kerr held out his wrists. Kovas seemed to get the message but hesitated. To drive the message home, Kerr said, 'I'd prefer to unbutton my own pants.'

The American transferred the Browning to his left hand, fumbled in his pocket for some keys and then, glowering at Kerr, unlocked the cuffs. He pushed Kerr roughly forwards into the heads compartment, 'Remember, no tricks or you'll end up as crab meat.' Kerr closed the door behind him, expecting it to be kicked open again, but it wasn't.

He dropped his pants, pumped ship and then sat down to cast his eyes round the compartment for some kind of potential weaponry.

Something practical. The toilet roll perhaps?

Maybe, but he'd need more than just a roll of paper. That, by itself, against an opponent armed with a Browning automatic pistol seemed too much like a one-sided contest.

He tried some lateral — De Bono style — thinking . . .

He cast round to look for something that at first glance might not be an obvious weapon but suitably modified could substitute for one.

As different ideas came to him, he evaluated their potential . . . The handle of the flushing-valve? Too short. The seat itself? No — he couldn't figure out how he could effectively use that. His eyes roamed back to the toilet roll . . . The toilet-roll *holder* might provide the answer.

He slipped off the roll of paper and carefully appraised the simple metal fixture. It had been manufactured out of a single chromed metal rod, then bent and contorted by a machine through various angles and fixed via two holes to a plate screwed fast onto the bulkhead wall.

Could he undo the work of the machine and straighten it out again to its original length? If he could — and with his imagination jumping ahead — he saw it as a potential weapon not too far removed from a military-style pig-sticking bayonet — albeit a blunt one.

Straightened out to its original length it could be a little longer than a modern bayonet and — handled with enough verve and force — probably just as lethal.

From the other side of the door, Kovas said, 'Come on, finish your shit. I've not got all day. I'll give you exactly thirty seconds to wipe your ass and that's it.'

Kerr found that the patent metal paper-holder easily unclipped from its bulkhead fixing. So far so good. Straining with his hands, he endeavoured to straighten out the various bends. He immediately discovered his bare hands had not got the kind of strength to undo the work of a press machine.

He paused briefly for more lateral thinking . . .

Then he realized that by using one of

the two fixing-holes in the wall plate as a vice to hold it at one end he could exert more leverage. It worked after a fashion. The result was a potential bayonet with several pronounced kinks remaining in it.

'What the hell are you doing in there?' The American's voice was now suspicious and threatening. At the same time he booted the door open and stood well back from it, pointing the Browning with an added menace. Kerr just had time to conceal his makeshift bayonet under his left armpit. 'Now, for Christ's sake, hitch up your pants and start moving.'

Kerr complied with the order.

'Hold out your hands,' Kovas barked, 'wrists together. I'm going to put those cuffs back. Remember, any tricks and you're crab meat.'

Kerr had long recognized the man was a mentally unstable killer — a psychopath with a hair-trigger temper. Best not answer back.

He saw the cuffs dangling in front of his eyes, in Kovas's right hand. He saw the automatic in his left. Ranby, he assumed, was back in the saloon or the wheelhouse. Except for that matter of the Browning pistol, it was a one-to-one contest.

Time was ripe for a showdown.

Kerr said, 'I'd like to wipe my hands first. Force of habit, see,' and he reached for the roll of toilet-paper. 'I'll be with you in a couple of seconds.'

Audaci favet fortuna.

'What the! . . . ,' exclaimed Kovas, taken by surprise as the loose roll of paper hit him square on his forehead, bounced off and unrolled itself further. Kerr realized the American had been only half distracted. Kovas had seen him reach into his left armpit and then whip out the crude weapon. Yet the American himself was fractionally too slow. As Kovas's fingers squeezed the trigger of the Browning, Kerr had already leapt for-wards and plunged the blunt metal rod through the American's shirt deep into the ample flesh of his soft under-belly. By the time the 9mm bullet was on its way, it was heading ten degrees off target, and Kerr heard it harmlessly splinter the pitch-pine woodwork behind him.

As Kovas, impaled, writhed on the deck, a second shot ran wild.

Then Kerr saw the writhing motion suddenly stop. Passively he watched while the eyes below slowly rolled up at him and remained transfixed with a disbelieving stare. A low gurgle escaped his throat. Then silence.

Kovas was dead.

Kerr snatched the Browning from the hand still firmly clutching it and moved quickly down the passageway leading back to the saloon.

He waited outside the closed door leading into the saloon for what seemed to him like an eternity before he realized that Ranby, who must have heard the shot, wasn't coming. At least not that way.

While he waited, the adrenalin thumped away at his temples. He'd just killed a man. He could still smell the fresh, sickly-sweet blood of his victim. He planned on killing another. He felt no revulsion at the prospect ahead. He was caught up in an atavistic surge. The veneer of civilization had been cast aside. Ten thousand years before, his ancestors killed brutally to survive. Kill or be killed! His genes inherited from one of those ancestors long ago still bore the same message.

Kerr knew Ranby was made of more cunning stuff than his American partner. Back in the saloon, it had been made clear that Ranby was the thinker.

While he waited, he tried to put himself in the Norwegian's shoes. He wouldn't go barging below deck, putting his neck in a noose. After the shots and rumpus, then that pregnant silence, he'd know something was wrong when Kovas didn't show. Now he'd be waiting somewhere for *him* to make the next move. Was he already exploring an alternative route for'ard to the heads compartment? There was bound to be at least one other way leading down through a hatch from deck level at the bow end.

Then it crossed his mind that if the vessel was anchored offshore, Ranby might have slipped over the side and gone for reinforcements?

He decided to wait another five minutes before making any exploratory moves himself. If the Norwegian had gone ashore to muster reinforcements, much of the advantage he'd gained in killing Kovas would be lost — unless, that is, he got himself up to the wheelhouse where he could watch any comings and goings.

But Ranby apparently hadn't gone ashore for reinforcements.

Kerr suddenly heard his movement above on the deck. After listening for several seconds, he judged Ranby was moving forward. It seemed to confirm there was a hatch leading down into the heads from the bow end.

Kerr gingerly opened the door leading into the saloon. As expected it was empty. Then he tiptoed through it and climbed the companion way which he'd earlier concluded led up to the wheelhouse.

Inside the wheelhouse there was no sign of Ranby.

There was still no sign of him when he raised his head sufficiently to peer through the wheelhouse glass towards the bows. He judged Ranby had now gone down into the heads.

Kerr started to take in his surroundings. The vessel — it *was* an old fishing-vessel — was anchored about 200 yards offshore in a small *vik* — a bay — in a wide branch of a fjord. The Dramsfjord? He couldn't be sure. Landwise he saw bare windswept rocks and a back-cloth of spruce woods, then more distant mountains. Lying just back from a narrow strandline, there was a solitary white- and red-painted clapboard house. There were two vehicles parked outside; he recognized them as late-model Mercedes estates.

Along the length of the strandline he noted several catwalk jetties. All had at least one *snekke* or a pram moored to them.

The total view was a picture-postcard set-piece. The kind favoured on Come-to-Norway travel brochures. An anonymous scenic cliché that could be anywhere along Norway's long and heavily indented coastline.

Maybe there was a chart in the wheelhouse that could provide a clue? In one of the drawers below the pilot table he found two charts — sheets numbered 3 and 4, titled Den Norske Kyst, Oslofjorden. He noticed erased pencil marks. They confirmed the probability the vessel was moored in the Dramsfjord, an offshoot of the much larger Oslofjord.

First sign that the Norwegian was still on the move was a faint creak of the door hinges in the direction of the companion way leading down into the saloon.

Kerr spun round and at the same time made a dive for the floor of the wheelhouse. On the way to the floor an angry wasp buzzed above his head and sped on to kiss and then shatter the glass of the wheelhouse behind him. Aiming the Browning, he blindly let off two rounds in the direction of the creaking hinges.

There were no answering thumps of bullets homing into flesh and bone. No yelps or groans. He knew his shots had gone wide.

Kerr stayed put on the floor of the wheelhouse, still aiming the Browning towards the doors leading below.

Several minutes passed by. He guessed

Ranby was dreaming up another ploy. Had he doubled back down the passageway and then climbed up to the deck again via that hatch at the bow end? Was he now waiting for him to show his face through the glass of the wheelhouse?

Ranby was most likely armed with an auto-weapon. If he raised his head, there'd be a burst of shots. At the distance from the bow back to the wheelhouse there'd be enough velocity for any bullets to penetrate the outer skin of pitch-pine woodwork and then do a lot of damage inside. Once he showed his face in the wheelhouse, Kerr knew he'd be vulnerable.

He waited another five minutes. Damn it! What was the Norwegian up to?

He crawled up closer to the doors leading down into the saloon and listened. He raised the Browning, aimed, and let off two quick rounds — shooting to hit anyone positioned immediately behind the doors. Then he cautiously pushed them aside for a view below.

The saloon was empty.

He now decided to chance a quick look

for'ard through the wheelhouse glass.

Ranby had gone over the side.

He'd swum ashore. Kerr saw him walking up the strandline and then start to head in the direction of the clapboard house.

The Norwegian was now hurrying. Furtively he kept glancing back over his right shoulder towards the fishing-vessel.

Ranby's hurry and his apparent concern with looking back triggered an ominous thought in Kerr's suspicious mind. He instantly recalled a dictum of his uniformed days when fighting terrorists: *If unexpectedly the enemy retreats, be prepared for immediate trouble!*

Acting on this dictum, Kerr wrenched open the wheelhouse door and then crawled out onto the open deck. He let the Browning drop from his grasp, slipped off his shoes and forward-rolled over the stern.

All the time he prayed he wasn't cutting it too fine.

20

' . . . You stupid bastard!'

Hines's face reddened, and the knuckles of his clenched fists were white. It was one thing being balled out by a department superior if you'd boobed, but not by a big oaf of a Viking.

In telling Eriksen about the call he'd made to Susie from the bedroom, he believed he'd been doing the right thing: you didn't run up expensive personal transatlantic calls on other people's domestic phone bills and not tell them. He'd wanted to pay out of his own pocket that kroner 60 charge the operator said the call had cost him. He couldn't believe Eriksen when he said that all transatlantic open calls routed from Oslo to Washington were probably tapped routinely by the KGB. The guy was seeing Reds under the bed. He was overreacting; he was like one of those obsessed hawks back in Langley. And, anyway, he'd not breathed a word to

Susie about Yankovsky. Who was going to be interested in listening to an American with routine domestic problems?

Eriksen had hit the roof, delivered some caustic oratory and gone straight away to look through the window into the street. He stayed at the window for about five minutes without uttering a word. Then he turned back to face Hines. 'Just as I thought. We've got company. Come over here and take a peek for yourself, but for crissake don't make it too obvious . . . See that shiny black Merc sedan parked just beyond the street-light? It's the Ivans. They know you're here.'

While the op was on, Eriksen's wife and their two offspring had gone to stay at her mother's place in the nearby suburb of Slemdal. Meantime Eriksen himself was playing mine host, major-domo, short-order cook and housemother to his American guest. The two of them had the house in Tidemands gate to themselves. Holmes was due in Oslo any time. Morgan Lucas would meet him at Fornebu and then drive him to another safe house in the suburbs.

Up to the time of the telephone episode, a friendly working cameraderie had been established between them, but now the atmosphere was tense. Eriksen, still glowering, seemed a million miles away, locked in thought. Suddenly Hines saw the Norwegian's set glower evaporate. A smile rose in its place. 'Okay, Hines, maybe that indiscreet phone call of yours wasn't such a bad idea after all . . . I've just had a thought. Here, have a drink while I explain . . . '

Eriksen's mood had apparently swung full circle. Inwardly Hines breathed a sigh of relief. While he and Eriksen had been looking in the street, he'd had time to think. He knew he'd boobed. Eriksen appreciated the local situation better than he did. He just hadn't thought it out before phoning Susie . . . Eriksen had been right to ball him out. The Agency's policy was right. An agent with domestic problems bugging him was liable to make himself look like some horse's ass. It could endanger life. Now, if what Eriksen said was true, he'd blown the whistle on a sensitive covert op. Maybe he'd resign

. . . 'Look, Eriksen,' he began in an apologetic tone, 'I guess you're right . . . '

'Forget it,' chipped in the Norwegian, cutting him short and gesturing with his hands, 'I might have done exactly the same in your boots. Listen . . . those Ivans staked out down the street have just told me the KGB haven't got any kind of clue where to start looking for Yankovsky. They're waiting there for one thing only . . . They're hoping *you'll* lead them to that deviate countryman of theirs. So here's what we do . . . '

21

All afternoon Kerr remained hidden above the opposite shore of the *vik* from where the house lay — watching events from behind a massive outcrop of weathered rocks twenty yards up the shore . . .

The balloon had gone up a fraction of a second after his body hit the fjord. He felt the blast from the explosion shudder through the water. Next time he dared raise his head and glance back, there wasn't much to be seen of the old fishing-boat. Nothing but a black pall of smoke and some floating debris.

Remnants of the smoke hung above the *vik* for several hours and must, he reckoned, have been seen from miles around.

After he'd scrambled ashore, he'd immediately concealed himself among the rocks. The house and the far side of the *vik* were still hidden under the pall of smoke. It was now time to put some of that military survival training to good use . . .

He'd stripped out of his wet clothes, squeezed out the excess water and laid them out to dry on the sunwarmed rocks. Then he'd indulged in some vigorous callisthenics to warm up. Fortunately it was one of those cloudless autumnal days when even in Norway the sun is still warm.

After the smoke began to clear, he could see the opposite shore of the *vik* and then the house. He noticed four men walk down to the beach, go aboard two prams and then row out to search amongst the floating debris. At one stage they actually rowed towards the outcrop, but none came ashore. In the end, the two prams returned to the far shore and the four men disembarked and walked up to the house again. This was a reassuring sign in his bid to stay free.

When he'd intuitively guessed that Ranby had triggered a hidden charge aboard the old fishing-boat, he'd evacuated the wheelhouse via the stern-facing exit. He realized that from the strand, the Norwegian wouldn't have seen him duck out. He'd kept low to the deck and then forward-rolled over the stern. He could assume now that Ranby and the others would be convinced their ex-prisoner had gone up in smoke just as the American's corpse had done.

As the hours of daylight passed, he watched several coasters conn up and down the narrow stretch of the fjord beyond the *vik*. When, for a time, one of the small vessels hove to and then lifted something from the water, he was too far away to make out what it was. Then, soon after, it was under way again.

Later he noticed a Volvo arrive on the far shore and then pull up at the house. After a brief halt it moved off again and continued down a track to the beach. It was a black Volvo; and when it turned and parked broadside on to his view, he could plainly read POLITI in bold white caps along its side-panels.

Two uniformed men got out and briefly looked across the *vik* towards the floating debris. One of the men from the house walked down, and the trio talked and gesticulated with each other for a few minutes. Apparently satisfied, the two policemen drove off again.

He saw no other movements that day.

★ ★ ★

When Colonel Stephan Zigel arrived in Norway, he was pleased to hear that the resident senior KGB agent — 'Cultural Attaché' Tanya Tereshkova — had made progress along several lines since he'd spoken to her a few hours before from Moscow. She had now established that the CIA agent Dr Jim Hines was ensconced in a private house in Tidemands gate, a short walk from Oslo's famous Frogner Park — home of the controversial Vigeland sculptures.

Men from the embassy were now watching the house round the clock. Tanya Tereshkova's research had already revealed that the private house was listed in the Oslo citizen's tax returns (open to all for public scrutiny) as occupied by one Reidar Eriksen, his wife and two children.

Eriksen was listed in another city directory as an employee of the Department of Overseas Aid. They couldn't expect Eriksen to be listed blatantly as a member of the PO. Not even the Norwegians with their obsession for open government would be stupid enough to do that. A line needed to be drawn somewhere. No matter, the name Reidar Eriksen of the Department of Overseas Aid was already in the local KGB files as a suspected member of the Norwegian Secret Service.

When Tanya Tereshkova greeted Colonel Zigel with a digest of news, she wore, he thought, a face like a cat who anticipated lapping cream.

'Good work, comrade,' he said formally. 'Your work will not go unnoticed by General Kerbel.'

'Stuff the general,' she said, maintaining her smile. 'It's good to see you again, Stephan. I'd already given up hope you'd ever wangle a trip to Oslo. I could almost give our aberrant friend Yankovsky a big Russian-style bear-hug.'

'Save it for me, Tanya. These last few

months alone in Moscow have given my appetite a keen edge.' He pressed his hands on her shoulders, bent his head and kissed her gently on the forehead.

'Mine too, Stephan,' she said, easing away after their brief embrace and then running her fingers provocatively over his semi-rigid loins.

'You play a familiar tune, Tanya. I find it very moving.'

'So do I, Colonel superior. Now off with the clothes! . . . State Security can wait. My own impatience matches yours.'

★ ★ ★

After the blood-red sun had dipped and the sky darkened over Dramsfjord, the air rapidly grew chill. Time now for the quarry of the day to emerge from their lairs to start hunting . . .

In Kerr's case it was a hunt for footwear. A man on the run without adequate protection to his feet is highly vulnerable to recapture. Mobility is the essence. Kerr had cast off his shoes before he'd abandoned the fishing-vessel in haste. Footwear of some kind was now his first priority; then he could think about trying to reach the safe house in Oslo.

The early evening moon, now waxing between first quarter and full, gave sufficient light for him to pick his route round the crescent-shaped strandline towards the house. The lights from the clapboard house shone like a solitary beacon in the *vik*. In the far off, fainter lights twinkled like distant stars; somewhere among them a farm-dog bayed to the moon. The nearest farm was probably several miles away; miles of painful walking which would surely cripple his feet. The condition of the hunter's feet was as important as his eyes. He'd have to try at the house first. There was probably some footwear in one of the outhouses. He knew from experience that many Norwegians kept their foul-weather gear in outhouses. His thin woollen socks would protect his feet from abrasions and cuts as far as the house, but not farther.

As he walked towards the house, he toyed with various plans for escape. He'd thought about the several prams and the motorboat moored on the catwalk jetties down by the strand. He ruled out the motorboat for several reasons . . . For one thing the odds were against him starting the engine in the dark without attracting attention. If he did decide to try to escape via the fjord rather than overland on foot, one of the prams would offer him a more silent means. A pram would be missed only next morning; by then — through the general — he could alert authority before Ranby & Co had time to escape the net.

Two hundred yards short of the house he stopped to listen for sounds of dogs inside. All day he'd listened from across the *vik* for the noise of dogs in the house; so far he'd heard nothing. All he could hear now was that distant farm-dog baying to the moon.

He reduced his distance from the house to within fifty yards. No howls responded from inside. The two Mercedes estates had remained parked outside all day. No one had moved in or out of the house since the police Volvo had left during the afternoon.

Stealthily he approached the house and then crouched below one of the heavily curtained windows at the front of it. He placed his ear to the clapboarding and listened. He could hear voices distinctly. Then he realized he was eavesdropping on a local radio programme. There were no other voices. The people inside were either listening to the radio or talking together in one of the other rooms.

Moving round the house towards the Mercedes estates, he had a sudden thought . . . He gently tried the driver's door of the first one. As he'd anticipated, it wasn't locked. Folk in country areas seldom locked doors of any kind.

He eased himself inside on the driver's seat and carefully clicked the door behind him. He immediately noted the keys dangling invitingly in the ignition lock. He resisted temptation. He hadn't planned on stealing the Merc. That could be a stupid move. It could raise an immediate hue and cry. The sight of those keys dangling in the ignition reassured him. If Ranby & Co hadn't believed he was lying dead at the bottom of the fjord with the remains of Kovas, they'd hardly have left those keys, would they! He wanted Ranby & Co to keep thinking that way as long as possible. First he needed a handtorch to help him find that footwear — that's why he'd decided to explore the Merc in the first place. As expected he found one in the glove-box.

Flashing the handtorch, he spotted some footwear in the back.

What he found wouldn't have been his first choice.

The rubber fishing-boots were lying under a large and rumpled waterproof sheet among a jumble of miscellaneous fishing-gear. They were green with fancy lace-up tops. He pulled them out and moved over into the passenger seat to give himself space to try them on.

Damn! They were at least two sizes too small.

He turned and rummaged about in the back again, but he didn't find any other footwear. He was now caught in two minds what to do next. There might be an alternative choice in the other Merc or in one of the outhouses . . . Then he recalled having seen something else in the glove-box when he found the handtorch — a sheathed hunting-knife. Best not to push his luck too far by searching the other estate or the outhouses. The hunting-knife might be the very tool to solve his problem.

Grasping it, he boldly carved out some rapid modifications to the toe of each boot — slashing them in a cross-pattern all the way through the rubber so his confined toes could stick out. The end result was highly effective and something resembling a pair of Roman buskings. As footwear they still left something to be desired, but they were practical enough to get him mobile and en route to Oslo.

He was still tying the laces of the boots inside the Merc when a sudden flood of light and then the clatter and bang of the house-door opening and closing heralded a quick change of plans.

He saw two figures had now emerged from the house and were approaching the estate. He could hear an exchange of conversation in Norwegian. He recognized one was Ranby. Kerr momentarily hesitated between two courses of action: Should he open the door and then make a straight dash for it into the night? or should he stay put? Even with this new footwear he didn't greatly rate his chances if it came to a cross-country chase — not if the two men were armed, which they probably were. The area immediately surrounding the house was too open to offer any effective cover. The spruce woods were at least a mile off. In the bright moonlight Ranby and his companion would spot him straight away. He expected they knew the local terrain intimately. He didn't. Even if he did succeed in outrunning them and then going to ground, they'd know for certain he'd survived the bomb on the fishing-boat. The covert op would be blown.

He recalled the large rumpled waterproof lying in the back. He could take his chances there and hide under it. Coming outside from the bright-lit house, they'd probably not see him lying in the back. Not at first anyway. Even if they did spot him, he could use the sheath-knife in defence. He could also use the handtorch to dazzle them. In the initial surprise, the advantage would be tipped his way.

In a split-second evaluation he weighed the choices ... After only a moment's hesitation, he flipped quietly over into the back and wormed his body under the waterproof.

Someone now gripped the door-handle on the driver's side. The door creaked open. From under the waterproof he glimpsed chinks of light creep in from the inside overhead courtesy lamp. He'd forgotten about that damned automatic courtesy lamp! Opening the door had triggered the switch. The inside of the Merc was now flooded in light! That light would stay on until the door was closed again. The lamp remained on. Had they spotted him? Adrenalin tautened his reflexes. He tensed, each hand gripping hard on the sheath-knife and handtorch, ready to spring to action.

★　★　★

An out-of-town police report about an old fishing-boat which had exploded on a lonely stretch of the Dramsfjord north of Svelvik found its way to E-Gruppa's headquarters in Oslo via the teleprinter. A few minutes later a copy came to rest routinely on Inspector Presterud's desk. When it arrived, he gave it only a perfunctory glance. He had no reason to associate in any way with the activities of James Kerr who now concerned his whole attention. The only thought to pass fleetingly through the inspector's naturally suspicious mind was the possibility of the boat's owner being engaged in an insurance swindle. However, it was not his problem *yet*. Just at this moment he had bigger things to occupy his thoughts. Nevertheless, when some six hours later the same teleprinter delivered another report that a body — or rather the headless and legless grisly remains of a male corpse — had been picked up by a small coaster in the Dramsfjord and then landed at Svelvik for a local coroner's examination, the inspector's interest was aroused.

It was aroused for three reasons.

Firstly, bodies of any kind found adrift

interested E-Gruppa. Secondly, the brief description of the body's condition suggested it was fresh and, in addition, the injuries inflicted on it could have been caused by a violent explosion. Thirdly, he recalled the earlier report about the fishing-boat: the owner of the boat had told the local police that no one had been aboard at the time.

Was that floating corpse a coincidence? Presterud decided to find out. He also initiated a news blackout on the report from Dramsfjord.

*　*　*

Ranby and his unknown companion were still talking. In reply to something he couldn't catch, Kerr, hidden under the waterproof, heard the Norwegian answer distinctly: '*Ja. Jeg vil komme tilbake snart.*'

At last someone was climbing into the driver's seat! Kerr sensed the movement via the sideways dip in the Merc's suspension. The door stayed open. From the drift of the to-and-fro talk it sounded as if Ranby were in the driving-seat. The Norwegian said to his companion: *'Hvis Yankovsky blir rastlös, gi han en spröyte til.'*

Who, Kerr wondered, was Yankovsky? The name was vaguely familiar. Yankovsky? . . . It had to be a Russian. It definitely wasn't a Norwegian name. What had Ranby meant about this Yankovsky being restless? Was the man injured? Ill? With a push, Ranby's companion finally clicked the door shut, and, mercy of mercies, the courtesy light switched off. In spite of the chill night air, Kerr's brow now dripped with nervous sweat. No matter, he'd passed the first hurdle.

The Merc stayed in rough washboard country tracks for several miles until, after slowing almost to a halt, he sensed Ranby make a full left turn. Immediately after, he felt the wheels glide onto the smooth silk of main highway asphalt.

Kerr still hadn't a clue about the Norwegian's destination. From time to time he heard the swish and rumble of passing traffic. As time went by, it seemed to grow more frequent. No vehicle overtook the Mercedes in the direction they travelled. Ranby, he could sense, kept his foot down for most of the time and frequently must have exceeded the 90km-per-hour top-speed limit. Occasionally he blared his horn impatiently, and Kerr could hear the almost continuous clickings of the headlight-dipping mechanism as Ranby flashed the slower traffic up front of him.

It must have been thirty minutes or so after they'd first hit the tarmac that the traffic became dense. Taking a chance, Kerr lifted the edge of the waterproof and peered out from under it. He recognized they were now entering a metropolis.

Drammen or Oslo?

It had to be one of those two with all those bright lights ... Yet if the Dramsfjord district was the place they'd left, by his reckoning they should have reached Drammen some time back.

Timewise the evidence now pointed to Oslo.

When they'd passed through three sets of traffic lights in one very short section

— Kerr glimpsed reflections from the sequences of red, amber and green — he knew it could *only* be Oslo.

He now faced the second hurdle. Where in Oslo was Ranby heading for? Where did he intend to park? He prayed when the Norwegian did park he wouldn't require anything from inside the back for his pressing engagement.

They were at a standstill. Before Kerr had time to realize it, Ranby had locked up and was gone. When he looked out from under the waterproof, the sidestreet was empty.

Then outside, Kerr couldn't quite believe his luck. Ranby had chauffeured him within five streets of his own destination in Oslo!

Wasting no time, he hurriedly crossed the busy Storgaten into Lybekk gate and noted passers-by cast him suspicious, curious glances. He realized that with his two-day growth of beard and unusual footwear he was attracting attention.

He prayed he wouldn't bump into a policeman who might ask questions.

He turned into Karl 12 gate. Outside a

block of modern apartments he paused briefly to scan the list of names. It was simply reassurance for his memory. Then, without hesitation, he pressed the appropriate buzzer of the entryphone numbered 5.

'*Hvem et det?* queried a tremulous female voice.

Kerr, recognizing the speaker, answered in English, 'A friend.'

'James!'

22

In the house in Oslo's Tidemands gate, Eriksen said to Hines, 'I want to get a good look at those two KGB heavies without them seeing me. So here's what I want you to do . . . Ever heard of our famous Frogner Park? In case you haven't, I'll give you a thumb-nail guide . . . It's our cultural Coney Island you might say, and you don't have to pay to get in . . . It's only a couple of minutes by shanks's from here. After you step out front, turn left. When you reach the first intersection — that's Gyldenlöves gate — turn right. Cross over Kirkeveien, and then it's straight in front of you — all seventy-odd acres of it. Have a good slow look around . . . it might just make you a little homesick when you bump into Abe Lincoln . . . His statue came courtesy of the citizens of North Dakota *circa* 4 July 1914. It's a popular spot for pilgrimages by visiting Americans so your going there won't make the Ivans too suspicious we're stalling them. When you've finished having a good look at old Abe, try those 150 groups of avant-guarde sculptures it took Gustav Vigeland, that countryman of mine, over 30 years to hack out. They're still a bit controversial. Not everyone's cup of tea — as the Brits would say. Hardly the place to take your maiden aunt from Connecticut — if you understand me.

'... When you get bored with the sculptures, try the Town Museum in the park and then, maybe, its restaurant or the cafe. If you do, ask for a slice of *blötekake* — soft cream-cake to you. It's our local speciality. They use real marzipan as topping ... I'll duck out first, via the fire-escape and then along my neighbours' roofs. I don't think they're watching the end of the street, yet. You wait — say four minutes — and then go out the front door nice and casual. I'll pick you up in the park — say in the open-air cafe in about two hours from now. Okay? Maybe then I'll have some hard news for you.'

★ ★ ★

Inside the Soviet Embassy in Oslo, Tanya Tereshkova, smiling contentedly, rose naked from the bed in her private apartment. She stretched her ivory, feline limbs in a luxuriant gesture. 'You haven't lost *your* touch either, Stephan. Like coffee? I've got a little of that Blue Mountain Special you always prefer.'

'I'm entirely in your hands, Tanya . . . ' answered Colonel Zigel with a salacious grin.

'I bet you say that to all your girlfriends. A *vazlyooblyennay* in every Soviet embassy, no doubt?' she replied teasingly, without malice.

'Only those comrades with an irresistible 38–24–36 layout like yours, Tanya,' he countered. 'That is if you'll excuse me using one of those dreadful vulgarisms I unfortunately picked up from the general's paper-backs.'

And she *did* have a superb figure, he thought, as he watched her from the bed busy herself in unashamed nakedness with preparations for his coffee. Tanya had domestic talents as well as those delightful corporeal ones. A perfect mate — perhaps also a perfect companion in intrigue? How long had he known her? Three years. They'd been lovers for only half that time. He hoped it was still the best-kept secret in the KGB. If the general ever found out, both their heads would roll — notwithstanding all their joint achievements performed in the service of the USSR.

She was the only one with whom he could relax and let his hair down — discuss serious literature, music and all those other finer things in life. She'd been a name only known to him on the files until they'd met on assignment in Copenhagen. Then he'd seen lust in her eyes; he knew there'd been lust in his own — unconsummated until chance brought them together again in Stockholm, out of sight of prying eyes. Since then there had been surprises for both . . . Yes, when they first met, it was what Maupassant had called *le rouge regard* — the thing which passes between man and woman when they are destined to fall in love. From the very start there had been more than simple lust.

He had fond memories of Scandinavia: Copenhagen . . . Stockholm . . . now Oslo. It might be pleasant to live in Norway — in Oslo? Pleasant to have a rich man's house in fashionable Holmenkollen near the big ski-jump and those evocative spruce forests all round you. Norway in many respects was very much like Mother Russia — but without all the necessity for day-to-day subterfuge on the part of its citizens. It wasn't Utopia, but by comparison with life in the Soviet Union it was the closest you could get to it. What would he do with his life if he ever left the KGB? Write? He would love to write. If he ever fell from grace in the KGB — and just a few days back he'd come very close to it — they would never allow him to join the Writers' Union. Without membership of the Writers' Union it would be quite impossible to earn a living inside the Soviet State.

Solzhenitsyn, of course, had written the truth about citizens' life — but only by going to the West had he retained his freedom. Western publishers had paid his countryman a vast fortune. What would they pay for the confessions of a long-serving KGB colonel who knew many of the unwritten secrets of the Soviet Politburo élite? . . . In his head he already had his title: *Twenty Years in the KGB*. It might one day head the bestseller lists in the American *Newsweek* . . . It would give him security to write those novels he'd long planned . . .

'A kopek for your thoughts, comrade,' said Tanya Tereshkova as she handed him his coffee. 'You were miles away, I think . . . Were you thinking about Yankovsky?'

'That man's name has not entered my thoughts for at least half an hour . . . Not since you dragged me off to your bed!'

'*Skatena!* — beast!' she cried. Then, when his own laughter died and his face suddenly grew pensive again, she brushed his cheek with her hand. 'What is it, Stephan? You look sad. Something is troubling you? The general? Do you suspect the general has heard rumours about us?'

'No. I don't think he knows, *yet*. But walls have ears, Tanya. One day our luck will run out. I have many enemies at Lubyanka. You should have seen all those faces when they believed I was due for the chop. Time is against *our* continued happiness.'

'Then, when the time comes, we shall defect ourselves, Stephan.'

It was as if she'd been reading his innermost thoughts.

'You'd agree!' he answered incredulously.

'I'd jump at the chance, *lyoobovnik* . . . if it meant we could be together all the time.'

Colonel Zigel stroked his paramour's hair. 'If we could find Yankovsky and take him with us, as a measure of our genuine good faith, I believe our welcome in the West would be assured. I do not think they would keep us incarcerated for long at Camp King.'

'Then we are of one thought, comrade lover!'

★ ★ ★

Inspector Presterud, his assistant Overn and a back-up crew of two forensics reached the old mortuary in Svelvik in under the hour.

When they'd all examined the corpse and after the two doctor/technicians had had ten minutes by themselves, Presterud called his own post mortem . . .

The man, without doubt, had very recently been involved in an explosion. It had *not*, however, been his cause of death. He'd been dead some minutes — perhaps for as long as thirty minutes concluded the forensic experts — when an explosion had ripped his body apart. Although the corpse was mangled: head, one arm and both legs missing, the two experts were both sure that the cause of death was a deep stab-wound made with a blunt instrument in the region of the lower abdomen.

'Jesus! Foul play then, chief,' said Overn aloud. 'Why couldn't this have happened last week. Just our luck when we're bogged down with all hands on deck looking for Kerr.'

'You're mixing your metaphors again,' said Presterud.

'Huh!'

'Our situation of being bogged down with all hands on deck sounds a bit ambivalent to me.'

'I wish I had your education, chief . . . but I guess you know what I'm driving at. Couldn't we pass this one over to the local CID?'

'Maybe,' answered Presterud, pensively. 'That tattoo on the remaining upper left arm interests me.'

' 'The Fighting 69th' thing you mean? Sure he could be a foreigner or a Norwegian who once served with an English-speaking outfit . . . Look, you don't think it's our friend Kerr, do you? Maybe he fought in an outfit called the 69th. We can check that . . . '

'It's not Kerr. The Fighting 69th are a US infantry regiment,' explained Presterud. 'They fought in Vietnam. I recall reading about them in *Newsweek*.'

'So you think this one's a Yank ex-soldier then . . . and you're curious to know what a badly mutilated body of a murdered Yank is doing in the Dramsfjord the same day we get a report of an explosion involving an old fishing-boat which is supposed to have no one aboard?'

'Tell the boys to get some prints from that remaining hand. The FBI might know the answer. We'll say it's urgent. Until we get word back, we'll hold off making any personal calls on that boat-owner, but tell the locals to keep a very sharp eye on that address we got. Now, let's get back to the smoke and start things rolling.'

23

Eriksen was already positioned behind the KGB Mercedes and hanging back in a doorway when he saw Hines walking down the street towards it. He saw confusion pass between the two watchers on the front seat and tried to imagine the what-shall-we-do-about-it playlet enacted between them.

One got out and started to follow the American.

It was Igor Granovsky. Eriksen had seen his mugshot — front and profile — a few days after he'd flown in to join the staff of the Russian Embassy as a so-called chauffeur. Some chauffeur! Strictly machismo. Six feet three inches in his socks; two hundred and thirty-odd pounds of solid bone and muscle. A weight-lifter's mass. The trapezius muscles on either side of his neck were bunched from regular bench press-work. Under the Russian's dark suit, Eriksen's

X-ray eyes saw hyper-developed pectorals, deltoids and triceps to match the rest showing above the waterline. A Soviet-built version of Mr Universe. The files on him back in the Department revealed no known history before he showed up in Norway.

When Hines disappeared round the corner in the direction towards Frogner Park, followed by Granovsky, Eriksen edged forwards to a spot where he could use his miniature binoculars to get a better view of the remaining Russian parked behind the wheel of the Merc.

Fadeyev . . . Yakov Fadeyev. No doubts at all. Another listed chauffeur; another grunt-and-groan Russian straight out of *Body Beautiful*. The files said there'd been a Yakov Fadeyev weight-lifter in the Olympics of a couple of times back. Consensus had it this was the same man — now put out to pasture. The Ivans at least looked after their own. And no square pegs in round holes either. Every man kept to his trade. The Ivans didn't believe in natural resources going to waste.

Eriksen backed down the street and hailed a *drosje*. 'Department of Overseas Aid, *takk*.'

In an office in the basement of the Department, a colleague greeted him. 'You've just had a personal phone call from Presterud of E-Gruppa. I said I'd get you to phone him back. Tried your house but no answer. Presterud sounded like a dog with a new bone.'

'*Takk*. Anything else?'

'*Ja*. We've scored with that known Mossad agent we've been trailing . . . He's been stalking a country place by the Dramsfjord . . . It's all in the report,' and he handed Eriksen a single type-written sheet. 'Funny, our colleague tells us the local police are also keeping an eye on the same address . . . An old fishing-boat has exploded — or was sabotaged — there. Maybe E-Gruppa are already into it — hence that personal phone call to you. Could get a little crowded down there in the Dramsfjord!'

Eriksen said, 'He's a real nosy bastard that Presterud. Too sharp by half. I thought our chief told his chief to tell him

284

to keep his outfit right out of PO business.'

'Maybe he doesn't know yet it's PO business. Maybe he suspects he might be walking into a minefield and wants you to confirm it?'

'You could be right about that, Björn. I'll ring him now.'

★ ★ ★

Colonel Zigel and Major Tereshkova had just returned to the Cultural Attaché's office in the main embassy building when the desk phone jangled. Major Tereshkova lifted the receiver . . . 'I see,' she replied, 'keep following and don't lose him.' She replaced the receiver and looked towards the colonel. She and the colonel had now assumed the masks of formal correctness. As Stephan had said: walls have ears. Even Tanya Tereshkova, senior resident KGB officer, was never sure about possible ears pressed to the walls (or doors) of her Cultural Attaché's office. In the privacy of the annex — in her bedroom — she felt safe, but never in the business section of the embassy itself.

'   ... The American Hines,' she announced, 'has made a move on his own. He is now casually strolling in Frogner Park like a tourist, apparently greatly interested in the finer points of those Vigeland sculptures. Granovsky is following him; Fadeyev has remained watching the house.'

'An inappropriate time for the American to be looking at sculptured nudes,' suggested the colonel suspiciously. 'Perhaps he knows we are watching the house and they've devised a ploy to shake us off.'

'I share the same opinion.' She bit her lip. 'The house in Tidemands gate has an upper-storey fire-escape onto the roofs of adjoining properties. The Norwegian Eriksen has probably already left by that way. I should have detailed extra men, but usually Granovsky and Fadeyev are very covert in their shadowing.'

'What auto did you use?'

'A black Mercedes as usual ... and before you raise more than an eyebrow, my dear Colonel, a black Mercedes parked in the streets of oil-rich Norway is as unobtrusive as a ten-year-old Moskvitch in Gorky Street.'

A suspicion of a twinkle entered the colonel's eyes. Tanya had spirit and was not inclined to take even a mild rebuke from her lover. 'Let's have a look at Hines ourselves, comrade,' he said. 'I have a feeling Eriksen has no immediate plans for meeting Yankovsky without Hines being present.'

Fifteen minutes later, arm-in-arm with cameras slung, the two Russians, like anonymous tourists, took up station between Granovsky and the man he was obviously shadowing.

There was no mistaking the American.

* * *

'Find out much about this Arne Ranby?' Inspector Presterud put the question to Overn when the sergeant got back from a trip downtown.

'Not a lot, chief. Except he's not really a local in the Dramsfjord district. He doesn't own that house either. I checked direct with the *kommune*. Tax-wise it's listed as belonging to Leif Nilsen . . . '

'*The* Leif Nilsen? The ex-mercenary? That neo-Nazi we've suspected of running drugs?'

'It caused me to arch an eyebrow too, chief.'

'How about that old fishing-boat then?'

'Yes, Ranby owned that all right, but it seems it wasn't insured.'

'Anything on Ranby's life-style?'

'The local police say he's supposed to have some odd friends . . . Come and go at all hours — so a neighbouring farmer, who lives down the track, tells them anyway. Ranby and his buddies keep themselves to themselves, as they say. Seems he's got a skipper's ticket. No form. Ex-blue-water sailor, but nobody locally knows how he makes his bread. Leastwise, he never went fishing in that old boat.'

'Check him out with the income-tax people?'

'Yep.'

'Well?'

'He's listed there as a consultant.'

'A consultant sailor? What kind is that?'

'Whatever kind it is, he makes good money. Paid tax on a declared income of 300,000 kroner last year. I even checked him out with the tax-evasion boys . . . No suspicion of any fiddles. His record sheet is lily-white.'

Presterud looked pensive and began to tap on his desk top with a pencil. 'There's definitely something funny going on down there in Dramsfjord.'

'I agree, chief. I don't believe in those kinds of coincidences either.'

Presterud was still tap-tapping away on his desk top in a metronomic rhythm. ' . . . First our friend Kerr decides to come running to Norway after supposedly killing a Norwegian citizen . . . Very odd that . . . Then this Hasler character goes missing on the *same* ferry from the Hook, and we now know from that FBI Telex we just had, he's definitely an ex-CIA dirty-tricks operator called George Brand . . . Then we have Kara Alstad murdered aboard the same ferry . . . A message passed down the line from the PO, via the Old Man, about keeping things under our hats . . . definitely no media publicity allowed . . . Finally, surprise, surprise — one of Brand's ex-CIA buddies, who's AWOL, suddenly turns up very dead in the Dramsfjord under highly suspicious circumstances . . . And now we come full circle and recall my original query apropos Kerr and our late colleague Sergeant Moen . . . '

'Why don't we just drop in on Arne Ranby, chief, and ask him some awkward questions? Like, for instance, those phone calls we've traced from that house to the ferry.'

'If we do, we might just be stepping on the PO's toes. We could be out of our depth on this one, but I wish those bastards in our very Secret Service could tell *us* a little of what's going on so we could keep our own books straight . . . ' Suddenly Presterud put down his pencil. 'While you were away, I rang that guy Reidar Eriksen who's supposed to work for the Department of Overseas Aid — just for a friendly off-the-cuff chat. He was out. What's his number again? . . . '

The phone on Presterud's desk jangled that instant. He lifted the receiver and then an eyebrow in the direction of Overn. 'Talk of the devil . . . '

24

'A very great American — yes,' pronounced the tall, handsome stranger at Hines's side. ''Government of the people, by the people, and for the people shall not perish from the earth',' the stranger continued — reading the bronze plaque's inscription below the imposing statue. ''Give me liberty, or give me death'.'

'That last quote's attributed to Patrick Henry,' Hines quickly corrected the man, '*not* Abe Lincoln.'

The stranger, smiling, answered, 'Yes — I know, but I think Lincoln might also have said much the same if Henry had not thought of it before him.'

Hines had noted that the stranger was tall, well dressed and distinguished in the European manner. He spoke English with a cultured foreign accent. He had a remarkably good-looking companion on his arm. His wife? Tourists? They were both hung with expensive cameras. Hines thought a more handsome couple couldn't have stepped out of the lead roles in a glossy Hollywood movie. Probably Norwegian or Swedish? Perhaps a little more Slavic-featured than most Norwegians he'd seen during his stroll through Frogner Park. But a lot of Norwegians, he'd noticed, *did* look as if they might be kissing-cousins to the late Uri Gagarin.

'Ever seen the Lincoln Memorial in Washington?' said Hines, warming to the stranger.

'I have not yet been privileged to travel to the United States. One day I should like to,' the stranger responded with a smile. 'Lincoln's views — on liberty in particular — have recently interested me greatly. I also like something else he once said: 'No man is good enough to govern another man without that other's consent' ... I find its message more agreeable than the ominous opinion of others ... '

'Like for example,' Hines suggested quickly, 'the one that says: 'It is true that liberty is precious — so precious that it must be rationed'.'

The stranger's eyes narrowed. He now seemed to look at Hines with more respect. 'You know your Lenin, then. I did not believe Americans *ever* read Lenin.'

'Not many actually do,' answered Hines with a grin. 'They don't read much about their own politicians, philosophers or poets either.'

' . . . For example, Robert Frost perhaps?'

It was Hines's turn to look with more respect. 'You've read Frost? I guess he's always been one of my favourite poets too.'

The stranger gestured with a dismissive wave of his right hand. 'I know a little of his work. His New England landscapes often remind me of . . . Well, never mind. I find him evocative. Please, will you join us in the cafe? Perhaps we could talk there about Lincoln and Frost while we drink coffee and eat some delicious *blötekake* . . . '

It was an invitation Hines couldn't resist.

★ ★ ★

'Listen Felix, I've got news. Can you meet me at Christiansen's Konditori in thirty minutes?'

Anders Tovalsen (Felix) was there in twenty-five.

While he waited, he ordered coffee and Napoleon's *kake* for two. He knew Ida Plevsky (Debra) had a sweet tooth.

She walked in exactly one minute before time.

'At Victoria Terrasse we've just had a Telex in from the FBI in Washington. E-Gruppa now know that Hasler was ex-CIA and his real name was Brand . . . They've also been told that the mutilated corpse fished out of the Dramsfjord was a man called Jake Kovas, a Vietnam veteran, ex-New York City Police and an AWOL CIA agent. I don't think they intend to let the Norwegian Secret Service know what they know . . . '

'Does Presterud think Kerr also killed Kovas?'

'I can't tell what he thinks. All I know is they still don't appear to know where

Kerr is holed up. That's the impression they give anyway.'

'Have you overheard the 'Friends for Peace' mentioned yet — by name, I mean?'

'No. I don't think any E-Gruppa people know that name at all. Was that telephone number and address I gave you in Dramsfjord any good?'

'You struck pure gold there, Ida.'

'The 'Friends for Peace'?'

'Could be it's the very spot they've got Yankovsky incarcerated. Maybe in the cellar . . . That's if he didn't also go up in smoke with Kovas in the old fishing-boat.'

'Let's hope not. When do you plan to move in?'

'Before E-Gruppa or the Norwegian PO decide to. Now E-Gruppa have found out it could be strictly cloak-and-dagger stuff, they might consult with the PO. Whatever, for us it will have to be tonight. You'd better get back to see if you can discover what their immediate plans are. Contact the embassy direct if you hear anything. They'll relay on to us. Looks like a busy time ahead.'

'Jesus, Hines! I can't leave you on your own for a minute without you dropping yourself right in it,' Eriksen was more exasperated than angry. 'Okay, I blame myself. I should have come with you as chaperone . . . Drinking coffee and eating cream-cake with the KGB's local top Mata Hari and her boyfriend in Frogner Park in broad daylight really takes the biscuit!'

'They picked me up, Eriksen,' protested Hines sheepishly. 'How was I to know? He sounded like a real nice, intelligent guy . . . '

'*Intelligent* is the operative word, for sure! What the hell did you talk about?'

'Abe Lincoln, Robert Frost, Lenin . . . This and that.'

'I just don't believe it.' Eriksen slapped his forehead with the palm of his hand. 'That guy with Tanya Tereshkova is probably one of the real top whizz-bangs at Lubyanka. It means they're pulling in all the big guns to look for Yankovsky.

He's most likely Yankovsky's ex-KGB contact man.'

'We didn't mention Yankovsky's name once. I swear it, Eriksen!'

'Jesus Christ, I hope not. Just think back now, calmly and coolly. What else *did* you talk about?'

'New England . . . and, like I said, this and that. Okay, so I've blown it again. How am I to know everyone round here's a KGB spy?'

'You're supposed to be on a covert op . . . not overt. Don't, I repeat, don't talk to anyone else. From now on you stick firmly in my sights. Lucky I came along to see what was happening before it was too late . . . How did those two Ivans take it when you got my signal to break it up?'

'They had their backs to you. I don't think they spotted you. I just glanced at my strap-watch and said it had been nice meeting them and now I had to be on my way.'

'You're sure that's all you said? I'm pretty good at lip-reading, Hines.'

'Okay, I might have said that if they're ever stateside, they could look me up. My name was in the book.'

'Jesus Christ! Now I've heard every-thing.'

★   ★   ★

'As we suspected, comrade, it *was* probably Eriksen himself who signalled to Hines in the cafe,' announced Major Tanya Tereshkova, examining the still damp photographic print. 'I am glad we sent off those extra people to watch events in Victoria Terrasse, just in case. See . . . ' she added, picking up the print and passing it across to the colonel. 'In this one we have both of them just after leaving the taxi. They must have taken a taxi to Victoria Terrasse immediately Eriksen picked up Hines in the cafe. The times check out.'

'Then we can assume rightly,' answered the colonel, 'they have brought in E-Gruppa for field-support. It looks as if they are making plans to move in on Yankovsky's captors. The problem is, Major, we still do not know *when* and *where*. If we cannot anticipate, we shall have no chance once Yankovsky is in E-Gruppa's hands.'

'As well as those photographs, Anton Sholakov had some interesting news for me in his report. He is one of my most promising students.'

'So?'

'He followed one of E-Gruppa's employees to a rendezvous — an assignation in Christiansen's Konditori . . . '

'Then you are operating a private detective agency on the side, comrade?' interrupted the colonel, raising an eyebrow.

'Patience, my dear Colonel,' she said teasingly, bending low and speaking sotto voce. 'All will be revealed in due course. Remember what our general is so fond of saying: leave no stone unturned, comrades, in your search for information . . . '

'The dénouement *please*, comrade, before I strangle you!'

'The subject Sholakov followed is female. She is a woman we have had on our local surveillance list for some time. We keep an eye on all known Jews in

Norway. Ida Plevsky was originally a Polish Jewess but is now a naturalized Norwegian. She is a graduate in economics. For some little time we have considered it rather strange that a woman with her obvious academic talents had got herself a job with E-Gruppa as some kind of communications clerk.'

'The thoroughness of your methods continues to impress me enormously, comrade, but time *is* short. Please tell a thickhead from Moscow what is the significance of your information.'

'We have suspected she *might* be an Israeli agent.'

'And now you are sure?'

'According to Sholakov, the person she met today in Christiansen's Konditori is a man known as Anders Tovalsen . . .'

'A good solid Norwegian name by the sound of it.'

'Yes, but a man with a Jewish mother. He is known to us as an import agent. Many of the things he handles come from Israel.'

'Still only *circumstantial* evidence, my dear Tanya, as those characters often say in the Western detective books our dear general so fondly reads for his edification.'

Again, sotto voce, she answered, 'Like I said earlier, Colonel, stuff the general. Sholakov was the star pupil at the KGB's special training school at Kalinin. Remember?'

'An expert lip-reader!' The colonel whistled under his breath. 'Now I remember the man. He lip-reads in English, German, French *and* Norwegian. Correct? Few comrades lip-read in Norwegian, that is why he was sent here on his first overseas assignment.'

25

'I feel honoured, chief,' grinned Overn.

'I'll reserve my feelings until we've closed the files on this one,' answered Presterud with a wary look.

'You think we might have been invited along as stooges for the PO?'

'You could be right. It could be the start of a beautiful friendship . . . Or it could be to make us look like smucks. Pay us back in full for Lillehammer. I'm frankly suspicious when the PO start to ask for our co-operation and help.'

'Maybe they just want to know where we are so we don't get out of step behind the scenes.'

'Nothing would surprise me, but they know we've got a vested interest and won't let go on this one. Nobody kills an E-Gruppa man and gets away with it . . . and there's a little matter of solving three or four other murders. Could be more before it's finished. But Kerr's still the real mysterious one. That house in Dramsfjord might hold the key to a lot of mysteries. Whatever, the PO will be reluctant to tell us *everything*. Remember, even in with them we'll still be left on our own to tie up the loose ends.' Presterud glanced quickly at his watch. 'Time to go. Hope you remembered to pick up your choice of hardware.'

'You bet, chief. I've drawn a Ruger 'three-five-seven with a shoulder holster and a Finlanda rifle with a 4x nightscope, plus flash suppressor. Ever see that movie *Sergeant York*? I might get a chance to exercise my prowess as a sniper.'

'Let's hope not,' answered Presterud uneasily. Trouble with Overn, he watched too many imported TV films. He was a good officer but prone to fantasising.

Kerr could clearly recall mounting the thick-carpeted stairs to the flat in Karl 12 gate. He could also clearly recall the door to the flat opening and seeing the frightened, blood-drained face of Anna peering round it. Then he'd had a fleeting glimpse of Ranby's face . . . Ranby! 'What the . . . ' he'd started to say to the

Norwegian. After that it was hazy as a blow sent him spinning into oblivion.

He could see Anna's face again now. Her drawn features slowly coming into sharper focus. She was bending over him. Her expression was one of concern.

'Who hit me, Anna?'

'The man called Arne Ranby. He arrived at the flat a few minutes before you did.'

'Ever heard of an ironical situation, Anna?'

'I do not understand, James.'

'Remind me to explain sometime.'

'You all right, James?'

'I think so . . . ' His eyes were now focused sharply and instinctively worked their way round the lighted room. He didn't see a window. Just a single closed door. The air smelt dank. The room was sparsely furnished and low. Not more, he estimated, than six-and-a-half feet from the bare concrete floor to the close-boarded pine-strip ceiling. Then, for the first time, he saw a second person. A man who sat inert, apparently half-dazed like himself. He was slumped in a soft-upholstered chair in a far corner of the room.

'Who's our friend? He looks vaguely familiar.'

'A Russian called Yankovsky,' she answered. 'He's still under sedation. I searched through his jacket pockets just after we got here. I found a plastic name-tag — the kind of thing used to identify people at conferences. According to that his name is Fyodor Yankovsky.'

Through the mists a bell rang. He knew he'd heard the name before. Those pictures he'd taken from Hasler's pocket fitted it. It was beginning to make sense.

He said, 'Where are we?' He knew it wasn't Anna's flat in Oslo — their safe 'house'.

'I've no idea, James, except it's obviously the cellar in a private house.'

'Whose house?'

'I don't know.'

'Where did ... the Russian come from?'

'He was already here when we arrived. You were unconscious; they blindfolded me for the journey. I'd say we were just short of one hour's drive from central Oslo. I checked my watch before they blindfolded me, then again immediately after they put us in the cellar.'

'Who are *they*, Anna?'

'I think they all belong to that Norwegian neo-Nazi connection of Brand's you and Olaf were hoping to uncover and smash.'

'Does the general know our cover is blown? Then you'd better tell me how Ranby got to know about our safe house.'

'Shortly after the general had phoned and told me Olaf was dead and your whereabouts was still unknown, I had two women callers at the flat. They told me on the entryphone they were collecting for charity. I told them they could come up . . . I was put off guard because they sounded and looked like very ordinary housewives. After they got inside, it was too late . . . The man Nilsen and two others suddenly appeared and then the women left . . . '

'I think I've met those same two,' said Kerr. 'They pulled a fast one over me too, Anna. But, go on.'

'Nilsen and the other two men searched the flat. Nilsen kept on questioning me about Olaf . . . Who was he working for? Why had he followed Hasler to Germany and Holland? . . . I told him I had no idea and I professed total ignorance as to what Olaf had been doing.'

'Did you convince them? Did they mention the SOC or the general?'

'Not a word about the SOC or the general. I think I was beginning to convince them I knew nothing . . . They kept at me all the time . . . asking the same questions. They said if I didn't tell the truth, a man would come who knew how to extract it the other way . . . Then Ranby arrived just before you did. Straightway he wanted to know what I knew about a James Kerr, an English friend of Olaf's. He said you were dead . . . Oh, James! First Olaf and then you . . . It was too much. I couldn't hide my feelings. They suddenly realized I knew more than I'd been letting on . . . Then you pressed the entryphone buzzer. They made me answer with a pistol at my head.

When I heard your voice and knew then you weren't dead, I couldn't stop myself from crying out. Ranby, I'm sure, was as surprised as I was. I couldn't warn you you were walking into a trap. After Ranby who'd been hiding along the corridor hit you and you were unconscious, I overheard him and Nilsen say that we would both provide useful hostages — if it came to that. Then I was blindfolded, and we were driven out of Oslo and brought to this place . . .

'Let's try and rouse the Russian, Anna. It's the only way we'll find out what's going on.'

26

Over Dramsfjord it was a clear, moonlit night. There was not a breath of wind. Cohen and Tovalsen had been in position lying up about a kilometre from the house since just after twilight darkness. Each wore a standard Israeli Army paratroop outfit, but without helmets or identifying flashes. Slung from their shoulders and belts were 9mm Uzi auto-machine-pistols, spare clips, British SAS-type anti-personnel grenades, and in Cohen's small valise three charges of plastic explosives he'd specially tailored up earlier that afternoon. All had been smuggled into Norway in diplomatic bags.

Cohen checked his watch. 'We'll go in exactly five minutes from now. Let's finish the coffee.'

While they drank the remainder of the coffee, Cohen said, 'You and Ida have done a good job.'

'Thank Ida mostly, Uri. Without her help we wouldn't have clinched it so quickly.'

'I know it, but don't forget it's teamwork which counts in the long run rather than solo performances. Let's not forget Hannah and the others. But I'm glad I decided to keep our numbers down on this one. That was the trouble as you know with Lillehammer. Talk about too many cooks spoiling the broth! It was like a guest-list at a Jewish wedding! And E-Gruppa knew exactly where to pick up most of our people. Very embarrassing it was. I'd like this current op to redeem our unprofessional track record in Norway. I want the boys in Tel Aviv to remember this in the same breath as Entebbe.'

'At least with Ida keeping her ear to the ground,' said Tovalsen, 'we'll get advance warning if E-Gruppa decide to come calling.'

'After we've let off some fireworks tonight,' said Cohen, 'there's going to be the local police, E-Gruppa and the PO swarming round the countryside like flies. Roadblocks . . . spot checks . . . the lot!

That's why I decided we'd slip in and out by sea using our small motorboat. Nobody is going to be looking for us on the Dramsfjord. Not immediately anyway. If we get Yankovsky in one piece, we transfer him under darkness to that yacht we have on hire lying off Svelvik and then go for a short cruise down the fjord. Even if they come knocking at the Embassy's front door, they'll find I'm on vacation and hopefully they don't know about you and Ida ... Right!' And glancing at his watch again, he said, 'Zero hour! Let's move it.'

★ ★ ★

The supporting team of local police were briefed by Presterud to remain back from the house at a discreet distance. Only if anyone tried to make a break and crash the roadblocks were they to enter the action themselves.

According to the local police, there was only the single dirt-track leading to the house from the main road. With this sealed off, Presterud was sure there could be no escape for the occupants except on foot or by sea. And even that latter possibility was already taken care of.

Eriksen on his part demanded that during the action Presterud must defer to him. That was the price for letting E-Gruppa in on *his* covert op. He wanted the shooting kept to a minimum. There was probably a Russian VIP somewhere inside the house. The PO and their friends wanted him badly; in one piece — *alive*. When Eriksen and his PO section got the Russian, they'd move out quickly, discreetly. It was then up to E-Gruppa to clean up the mess and attend to any formal paperwork. Eriksen said he didn't want the PO's name mentioned to the media . . . As Presterud and Overn had both first suspected, one reason at least for Eriksen including E-Gruppa was he was going to unload onto them the problem of handling the media when the dramatic story broke about gunfire and possible mayhem in Dramsfjord.

Presterud had reluctantly agreed to the bargain. As far as he knew, this mysterious VIP Russian had so far committed no offence against the Norwegian State.

The combined E-Gruppa/PO assault team arrived at Dramsfjord just before sunset and parked their vehicles two kilometres back from the house. They remained well hidden among the spruce woods.

They started to move in towards the house thirty minutes after darkness had fallen, guided over the open, flat expanse immediately surrounding the house by the light of the early-evening moon . . .

Eriksen and Presterud had agreed to limit the number of the assault team to eight — four from each. More than that and they could start to get under one anothers' feet. If reinforcements were needed, the local police could quickly move in to assist. They were armed too.

E-Gruppa's contingent consisted of Presterud, Overn and two constables (Willy Loften and Gunnar Gjertsen). Like Eriksen's PO team, they were dressed in Norwegian army assault overalls. All wore British-made '2Z model' lightweight body-armour vests designed to withstand a burst of submachine-gun fire at close range. All were armed and trained crackshots.

Presterud himself carried a 'thirty-eight police model Smith and Wesson with a short barrel. It was the handgun he'd joined up with. It was the most reliable handgun he'd ever used; those fancy modern automatics sometimes had a nasty habit of jamming at a crucial moment. Even with the short-barrelled, less accurate, version of the standard S & W 'thirty-eight, it was possible to drop a man lethally, if need be, at 25 metres. Tonight, any longer-range stuff he'd leave to Overn and constable Willy Loften who was also armed with a Norwegian-made Finlanda rifle — probably, he mused, the most accurate rifle in the world. For handguns both constables had drawn from the armoury 9mm Parabellum Browning automatics with Luger-style 13-shot magazines. E-Gruppa allowed its officers a wide choice of weaponry. It was appreciated everyone had their individual quirks when it came to choice of guns as personal survival depended on it. Presterud noted the younger officers usually opted for auto handguns. It was to be expected since they looked more glamorous and could fire more rapidly and therefore had a better image. Presterud, with his long experience, knew different. It was *experience* not rate of fire which counted in a close-encounter shoot-out when the chips were down.

Presterud's professional eye noted disapprovingly that Eriksen's team all carried fancy secret-service issue double-action 9mm Parabellum Berettas — model 92 DA — with 15-shot magazines and smooth, black plastic handles. One thing Presterud couldn't abide was those modern-age plastic-handled guns!

In addition both sections were equipped with smoke masks and UHF radio transmitters through which all could keep in touch — including, if need be, the supporting team of local police remaining back at the roadblocks.

Eriksen had introduced his three companions simply as Jim, Morgan and

Björn — purposely omitting their surnames. Presterud at least recognized Björn Olsen, another PO man he knew operated incognito at the Department of Overseas Aid. He didn't recognize the other two who'd just nodded back when introduced. Then he overheard them speaking English among themselves. Americans . . . CIA? That's why they had strangers' faces. He hoped to God the two Americans knew how to handle themselves in a rough-house when the lead started to fly. It was obvious, of course, they came with Eriksen because of the unnamed Russian VIP inside the house. These were 'the friends' of the PO Eriksen had spoken about.

Presterud and Overn also carried some smoke-grenades and two auxiliary battery lamps — the grenades to be used only if absolutely necessary. Presterud, in addition, carried a bull-horn loudhailer strapped round his neck to address the occupants of the house in the event the attack subsequently developed into a siege . . . A siege was the last thing Eriksen wished to get involved in. The

317

plan was to approach the house in darkness using stealth, make a surprise forced entry, identify and then grab the Russian and at the same time hopefully disarm the rest inside.

Whoomf!

The unexpected blinding flash and explosion at one end of the house instinctively sent the E-Gruppa/PO assault team horizontal and face down to the ground.

They were still 1,500 metres short of the house.

The lights of the house suddenly went out. There were several intermittent bursts of small-arms fire. Then it was silent again.

'What the hell!' exclaimed Eriksen to Presterud lying alongside him. 'The bastards must have spotted us already.'

Presterud now had his binoculars focused and was scanning the house. Somewhere in the distance a spitz dog bayed to the moon. It took time for Presterud's eyes to recover from the blinding flash of the explosion. 'Something funny's going on down there,' he said, voicing this thoughts aloud to Eriksen. He could barely believe his eyes as he glimpsed three figures — two apparently dressed in combat gear and clutching autopistols — plunge out through a gaping hole in the side of the house and disappear into the gloom. From the house, another burst of small-arms fire followed their exit.

'Listen,' he said to Eriksen, who was now busily focusing his own binoculars. 'Had you been expecting competition?'

The truth dawned instantly on Eriksen. 'Jesus! Let's go in and see what we can salvage. Alert the support boat.'

Presterud spoke briefly through his UHF microtransmitter and then switched off.

When the assault team got within 200 metres of the house, Eriksen ordered them to stop and fan out. Everyone was to remain back from the house at a discreet distance. Eriksen nodded to Presterud. Presterud detailed his two constables to move round to cover the rear of the house. No one was to start shooting unless in self-defence or unless

Eriksen or Presterud specifically gave the order.

All was quiet inside. The house lights stayed off. Presterud's radio bleeped. Willy Loften said, 'I'm in position, chief. We've got the back covered now.'

'What do you think?' said Eriksen to Presterud.

'I think we could be too late, but I wouldn't like to bet on meeting passive resistance inside that house *now*. How about me using the loudhailer?'

Eriksen reluctantly agreed.

'This is the police!' shouted Presterud in Norwegian. 'We've got you surrounded. Come out with your hands raised. We shall give you exactly thirty seconds.'

Then he bleeped Willy Loften and, speaking into his micro-transmitter, ordered, 'Lights, Willy.'

The back of the house was suddenly lit by the portable siege lamp; Presterud switched on his own and then positioned it on the ground. The house was now effectively illuminated front and back. Presterud knew the lightweight nickel-cadmium batteries were good for half an hour. He expected to have the operation sewn up a lot sooner than that. Eriksen had apparently got his timing wrong, but that wasn't his problem.

Inside the house there was no sign of movement. The spitz in the distance bayed another solo. After a five minutes' stalemate, Presterud used his loudhailer again and repeated the earlier instruction.

Still no response.

'I'm going in,' said Eriksen. 'I want that Russian alive. Some poor innocent bastard might be bleeding to death or something. You're absolutely sure you saw only three people duck out? They could have been an Ivan assassination squad.'

'I'll come with you,' said Presterud. 'I'll cover your back. Remember, Eriksen, this is supposed to be a joint op.'

Eriksen grinned back at Presterud. 'You boys don't like being left out of the limelight, do you, Inspector. Okay, as you say, it's a joint op, but I'm still supremo — remember.'

Eriksen, gripping his plastic-handled Beretta in his right hand, moved forward into the pool of light. Presterud followed, nursing the familiar antiquated wooden handle of his thirty-eight. He followed ten metres behind Eriksen.

Eriksen reached the side of the house without incident. He paused, pressing himself against the white clapboarding as if to gird his loins before entering through the ragged gap torn in the outside walls to his left. Presterud was still a few metres out from the side of the house. He felt exposed and vulnerable. In the distance the spitz crooned again to the moon and made him pause. For the first time that night he was distinctly jumpy. A frisson of fear ran down his back. It was then, as if alerted, he heard the faint but distinct scrape of something moving above his head inside the darkened house. Instinctively he started to arc and drop into a marksman crouch to meet the direction of the sound, at the same time raising his gun arm. Before his arm had orbited half the necessary swing distance, he heard the hard crack of a Finlanda rifle exploding behind him. There was a tinkling of glass confused with the thump of a high-velocity round striking flesh and then pulverizing muscle and bone. Uninjured, he sprang to the shelter of the side of the house and pressed himself against the clapboarding. His palms felt cold and clammy. His radio bleeped. 'You okay, chief?' It was Overn. 'I got the bastard. That upstairs window was just ajar. I think I see the shadow of another . . . '

Even before Overn finished, a burst of small-arms fire rang out from inside and one shot ricocheted off the portable siege lamp. Before the whine of the ricochet died, the Finlanda answered. There was more shattered, tinkling glass — another interconfused lethal thud. Presterud's radio bleeped again. 'Got him too, chief. Looks very quiet inside now.'

'Thanks — '

'Think nothing of it, chief. Easy as shooting fish in a barrel — as the saying goes.'

The house lights suddenly flashed on. Another bleep on the radios. This time it was Eriksen's voice. 'Okay, folks. I'm inside. The show's over. Hines, I'd like you inside pronto to identify some corpses.'

27

There were four corpses for Hines to scan. He'd seen many corpses before. People who'd died violent deaths. An indoctrination course designed to expose trainee agents to looking at people who'd met death violently was all part of the CIA's basic training. Two of his class-mates had opted out. They couldn't stomach the sight of spilt blood and always brought up. Like those who never get used to the roll of a ship, there are those who can't get conditioned to staring violent death in the face. Hines heard later they'd both joined the Revenue Investigation Service. Looking at balance sheets could still be hard on the eyes, but it was a darned sight easier on the nerves.

It didn't pay to exercise too much imagination. Hines discovered early on that the trick when examining corpses was to adopt the strictly detached, clinical approach. Look at a corpse the same way

you'd look at a stuck heifer or a pig.
Think of the morgue as a kind of human
abattoir . . .

Two of the corpses were on the ground
floor of the house; two upstairs. The ones
upstairs had only just stopped bleeding.
All had been fatally shot. All were armed
with deadly Heckler & Koch submachine-
guns — the favourite weapon of the
urban guerilla. At the sight of those
German-built weapons, Eriksen guessed
they were all ex-Baader-Meinhof jobs.
Now none of the assault team had any
qualms about the killings.

None of the corpses was Yankovsky's.
Hines was absolutely sure about that.

Presterud's UHF radio suddenly
bleeped.

' . . . You're sure . . . ' he said, after
listening to the message. 'Nice work,
anyway, Thor. I had a feeling someone
might try to slip out by the back door
. . . We'll meet you down at the strand
and sort it out for you . . . Sure, I'm as
confused as you are. I think Eriksen
knows the answers . . . He'd better!'

Presterud then bleeped the local police

waiting back at the roadblocks. 'Get our vehicles up here, and do hurry it! We're now on our way down to the fjord to rendezvous with *Oslo Queen 2*.'

Then he turned to Eriksen. 'You heard what Thor Gardal said. They've picked up quite an assortment . . . a couple of gunmen, a Norwegian girl and apparently two strange Russians — one male, one female . . . and the whole bunch of them are protesting like hell! He's confused like me!'

When the eight-man E-Gruppa/PO assault team arrived at the fjord edge, the prisoners were all assembled and under armed guard in the large midships cabin of E-Gruppa's high-speed support vessel *Oslo Queen 2*, now tied up at one of the catwalk jetties.

Down below, Eriksen straightway recognized Uri Cohen and Anders Tovalsen. The recognition was mutual. A few seconds later he recognized the cultural attaché at the Soviet Embassy and her tall companion he'd seen in Frogner Park. Presterud, in turn, was sure he recognized the very three persons whom he'd seen leave the house after the explosion.

Inspector Thor Gardal, Officer-in-Charge of *Oslo Queen 2*, quickly related to Eriksen and Presterud how just shortly before he'd intercepted and detained a motorboat carrying Anna Solberg and four other persons, two of them purporting to be members of the Soviet Embassy in Oslo and now claiming diplomatic privilege.

Uri Cohen said, 'Listen, Eriksen, we've got to get through to you. I'm acting as spokesman for all of us.' He gestured his arm to include Anna Solberg, Tovalsen and the two Russians. 'Get this craft of yours heading downstream *full fart* towards the Oslofjord. I'll explain how things are as we go along. If you don't act immediately, you'll be sorry, I promise you.'

'Where's Yankovsky?' asked Eriksen suspiciously.

'That's exactly what we all want to talk to you about. Move it man!'

Eriksen rubbed his chin, then looked at Presterud and nodded.

Presterud said to Thor Gardal, 'You

heard what the man said. Move it
... *Full fart!*'

Oslo Queen 2's twin-500 HP diesels
roared to life. The helmsman manoeuvred
away from the catwalk jetty and swung his
helm. The bows lifted towards the open
water to the south.

Inside the cabin, Uri Cohen turned to
Anna Solberg. 'Tell Eriksen what you told
us, Anna.'

Breathlessly she began, ' ... Yankovsky,
the Russian, is being held by a group of
Norwegian terrorists. We were all, that is
James ... James Kerr, Yankovsky and
myself, held prisoner in the house ... I'll
explain later how we got there ... '

She'd seen puzzlement reflected in
Eriksen's face and the faces of the rest of
his party.

' ... Anyway, James and Yankovsky
were taken away by the one called Arne
Ranby and another man called Leif
Nilsen ... I'm sure — on a boat
— somewhere. You see, back in the house,
Ranby and Nilsen and the others
suddenly became jumpy. I think they had
seen some strange lights moving offshore

in the *vik* — it was perhaps the lights of this vessel. I heard Ranby tell the others I was to remain back at the house as a possible hostage while he and Nilsen would take James and Yankovsky out into the fjord. It was implied that James and Yankovsky were also going to be used as hostages if it became necessary . . . '

'What Anna is trying to tell you in a nutshell, Eriksen,' interrupted Cohen impatiently, 'is that Tovalsen and I blew our way into the house back there looking for Yankovsky. All we got was Anna and to get her we had to shoot a couple of guys who got in the way. We left the rest upstairs somewhere because Anna mean-time told us that Yankovsky had been taken away just before . . . We then hotfooted it back to our own *snekke*, taking Anna with us . . . Unfortunately we were jumped by our two Russian friends here. They'd watched us attack the house; and when they saw *three* of us come out, they thought we had Yankovsky in tow. To cut a long story short; when they discovered we'd come out empty-handed, we agreed to co-operate, temporarily. You see, we both found we had the same objective in mind — friend Yankovsky . . . Yes, you can raise an eyebrow, Eriksen. Whoever heard of a joint Mossad-KGB op! Well, it's happened tonight. Because ours was the more powerful craft, we all decided to use that. Unfortunately, in turn, we ran slap-bang into *Oslo Queen 2* here and were jumped by your ever-zealous Inspector Gardal who wouldn't act on what we told him until *you* came along . . .

'Now, what I was trying to explain to the inspector when you arrived was that time's running out fast for *all* of us. The thing that worried me was finding out from Anna that those two hot-heads, Ranby and this other man Nilsen, had got Yankovsky in tow. Those two will now most certainly know the whistle is blown on them . . . If my hunch is correct, they've decided to go ahead with a certain threat they were paid by some Middle Eastern friends to execute. The man pulling the strings — Peter Hasler — I'm pretty certain never intended to do it because he was hatching other plans, but

I'm sure the rest of his organization didn't know what he was up to. Right now they're out there in the fjord — heading for a rendezvous with several packages of highly lethal Soviet ironmongery — which the colonel here has vouched for is definitely out there somewhere. It's no bluff. Before anyone can raise another finger to stop them, Yankovsky is going to be forced to press all the appropriate buttons on a gadget he's devised himself . . . Now my problem is *I* don't know the precise location of those packages of ironmongery . . . '

Eriksen turned to Jim Hines and Morgan Lucas. 'Either of you two know exactly where those missiles are parked? Let's try to plot them on the chart.'

Hines shot an uneasy glance at Morgan Lucas. Morgan Lucas as spokesman answered, 'Only approximately. I don't have the exact coordinates on me right now . . . '

'Shit!' exclaimed Eriksen. 'Then we could be in big trouble. In daylight we could get half a dozen choppers up and spot their boat. No sweat. By dawn it could be too late. Tomorrow, if any of those missiles go up, Norway and Israel are going to make world headlines in every newspaper — that's if by then anyone's left around on this planet to print them!'

'I know *exactly* where they are.' All faces swivelled immediately to the tall Russian colonel. He unbuttoned a jacket pocket, removed a slip of paper and scanned it. 'Please, a chart of the fjord, quickly.'

28

As Kerr slowly came round, he had the impression he was staring up at the moon from the bottom of a deep well whose walls were gyrating above him. Then he sensed from the motion and the sounds he was aboard a motorboat travelling fast over smooth fjord-water.

He lay quiet, barely opening his eyes. He was lying in the stern end. His wrists were bound, but his legs were free. Looking for'ard, he could see three figures huddled in the protection of the midships cockpit. In the bright moonlight he recognized one was Yankovsky. The helmsman was Ranby . . .

What the hell was going on? He decided to lie doggo until he could think straight again. His head was spinning like a fast-rotating centrifuge, and the throb of the powerful diesels alongside him didn't help his fragile condition.

He gauged the motorboat was around

40 feet long. It was definitely the same motorboat he'd seen moored earlier at one of the catwalk piers. From the roar of her twin diesels and the general tilt of her bows, she was a fast mover. He estimated their speed was about 35 knots . . . maybe even more. He could see shore lights immediately pressing in either side of them. From the position of the moon, he saw they were definitely travelling south. He guessed they were still in the narrower Dramsfjord and the open stretch of the main Oslofjord lay ahead of them . . . They were obviously going somewhere in an almighty hurry.

His dazed brain now slowly began to recapitulate recent events . . . He recalled the house in the *vik* — back there in the darkness — where Anna, the Russian and he were being held prisoner . . . How Ranby and Nilsen had come to the cellar, and then the Russian and he had been separated from Anna and hustled outside and down to the beach and forced aboard the motorboat at gun-point . . . Afterwards, inexplicably, there'd been the blinding flash and the large bang of an explosion followed by the intermittent rattle of smallarms fire from the direction of the house. Soon after there'd been an exchange of excited conversation on the motorboat's radio . . . He'd then realized *someone* was attacking the house . . . He recalled his own frustrated attempt to take over control of the motorboat when Ranby and Nilsen were momentarily distracted by events back on shore . . . That's when Nilsen must have clobbered him . . . Blackout.

But he recognized his brain had moved forwards too fast. There was something else . . . Something Yankovsky, the Russian, had told Anna and him . . . Now he remembered . . . Yankovsky had related all the events of his recent kidnapping in Holland . . . *This was what the whole episode was all about!* Yankovsky admitted he was a frustrated homosexual. He believed the KGB had been suspicious about him. He said he'd intended to defect to the Americans at the end of a conference he'd been attending in the Hague . . . Peter Hasler and the man called Kovas had surprised and photographed him in a compromising situation in a Dutch brothel . . . He'd been so confused; because they said they were police, he'd left quickly with them . . . Then later Hasler told him he was a CIA man and was taking him to a safe hiding-place as the KGB's assassination gangs were after him . . . He'd been very frightened . . . He'd told Hasler and Kovas all about Admiral Gronika's Silent Men missiles . . . He'd brought this information to the West in good faith to use in exchange for political asylum and eventual citizenship and academic status in the United States . . . Then Kovas, who spoke Russian like a native, had told him what was expected of him . . . They'd brought him to Norway . . . They wanted him to fire those missiles at Dimona in Israel! Kovas threatened more torture if he didn't comply . . . If someone looking for Yankovsky had attacked the house, Ranby and Nilsen would know that time was running out for them.

My God! The implication of that last thought hit him like a cold douche and cleared his brain. The motorboat, he'd already surmised, was travelling fast. On its way, was it, to the site of those Soviet missiles in the main fjord? That *must* be their plan. It was clear that Ranby and Nilsen were still intent on firing those missiles at Israel!

He could probably raise himself and move about, but with his wrists bound, he'd be next to useless in tackling Ranby and Nilsen, who were both armed. The painful echoes of the blow from Nilsen's pistol-butt still rang inside his skull.

Trying to tackle two armed men with his wrists bound would be foolhardy. If he could get in at close quarters, he could use his feet in some adroit kickboxing. In an unconfined space he could use those feet of his very effectively, but could he in the confines of the motorboat's cockpit?

How much could he count on Yankovsky's physical help? Not much, he reckoned. The Russian's body wasn't built that way. What's more, it had been apparent back in the cellar his will to resist had been broken by sedation and threats. The horror to be faced was that in the hands of Ranby and Nilsen, Yankovsky would comply with their bidding. Back in the cellar, Yankovsky had explained his black-box apparatus for firing the four missiles was childishly simple. He'd carried his small apparatus to the Hague Conference to show to the Americans when he defected . . . He planned to contact an American he knew called Larry Holmes on the very last day of the proceedings there. But Holmes had left the conference the day before . . . Not until he was in Norway, incarcerated in the house by the Dramsfjord, had he realized he'd been kidnapped and tricked by Hasler and Kovas. They'd used torture and sedation to break him.

No, from Yankovsky, Kerr realized, he could not depend on any help.

First task was to break his wrist-bonds. He cast his gaze round for something suitable . . . What about the metal canopy covering the twin diesels? Pressed steel plate a quarter-inch thick with rounded arrises. Not exactly any sharp cutting edges but nevertheless a tool of a kind. There was, however, going to be pain every time his flesh touched the bare hot metal. It would be slow work. He wasn't going to be able to actually cut those bonds securing his wrists. They felt like heavy-gauge nylon fishing-line which had dug deep into his flesh. Friction and heat were his only means . . . Nylon, he knew, was susceptible to friction and heat. He could generate frictional heat by rubbing. He could glean *direct* heat from the metal of the diesel exhausts. The former was less painful; the latter more effective. He tried to remember the melting-point of nylon. Whatever it was, he knew it was above the temperature that scorched human flesh.

Rub, rub, rub . . .

How much time had he got? He tried to conjure up a mental map of the main part of the Oslofjord — the lonely 20-kilometre reach of open water stretching from Holmestrand on the west bank to Moss on the east.

. . . *Rub, rub, rub*

The shore lights receded. The motor-boat was now moving out of the Dramsfjord into the main Oslofjord. How close to those missiles did they intend to get before making Yankovsky perform with his magic box of tricks?

. . . *Rub, rub, rub*

Jesus, he could feel and then smell the burning flesh as his wrists and hands blistered and fried. He grimaced in pain. It made him forget the hurt in his head. The stench of scorching human flesh was up in his nose now, making him retch. That stench was something you never forgot. He'd first smelt burnt human flesh when the IRA had blown up one of his unit's trucks — and five companions were cremated to cinders in the holocaust.

. . . *Rub, rub, rub*

He could have screamed out in pain. By the time he'd got rid of those nylon bonds, his hands would be useless to fight with. How he would have liked to plunge them overboard to assuage the pain in the cool fjord-water.

. . . *Rub, rub, rub*

The vessel had started to lose way. They were arriving in position. His wrists remained fettered.

. . . *Rub, rub, rub*

As the rumble of the twin diesels died away, he could hear Ranby and Nilsen talking to Yankovsky. Yankovsky was hunched over his apparatus. The Russian was going to co-operate all the way!

'Don't do it, Yankovsky!' Kerr shouted. 'Don't do it, man!'

He saw Yankovsky turn his head to look back in his direction. It was too dim for him to see the expression registered on the Russian's face.

. . . *Rub, rub, rub*

Kerr saw Nilsen start to move back towards where he lay.

. . . *Rub, rub, rub*

Suddenly, to the far side of Nilsen, there was a flurry. Kerr heard Ranby call out in Norwegian, 'Stop him, the bastard's going overboard!'

Ranby whirled round and made a grab towards the Russian. He missed. Kerr heard a splash. Yankovsky was over the side, now thrashing about in the fjord.

'There he is!' shouted Ranby in Norwegian. 'Pass me the boathook, quick! . . . Blast the bugger — he's gone under. Get the lights on!'

Lights suddenly flooded the cockpit of the motorboat and the fjord round about.

'Here he is!' shouted Nilsen, indicating over the port side.

'Got the sod!' exclaimed Ranby. 'Give me a hand to haul him back on board.'

. . . *Rub, rub, rub*

Kerr saw them drag Yankovsky back on board. He heard Ranby say in his heavily accented English, 'Don't try that again. Now, action! Understand that?'

'Don't do it,' Kerr shouted again.

. . . *Rub, rub, rub*

'Shoot that bastard back there!' Ranby ordered Nilsen.

Kerr saw Nilsen raise his arm and take aim with his auto-pistol. It was point-blank range. He couldn't miss.

From somewhere behind, Kerr heard the crack of a rifle. He saw Nilsen's face suddenly set with a puzzled, dazed frown . . . Saw — as Nilsen hovered above him — something dark stain and gush from his chest. Then, as Nilsen sank to his knees, he cried out to Ranby, 'Lights . . . Turn off those bloo . . . d . . . y Li . . . g . . . hts.' Flecks of scarlet dribbled from his mouth. Losing balance, he toppled forward on his face and lay in a heap, gurgling vomit and blood.

Ranby seemed momentarily paralysed at the sight of his dying partner, then recovered. Kerr saw his hand shoot out towards the switch, and the motorboat was plunged into darkness again. An instant later another rifle-shot smacked at the superstructure, then whined and richocheted, smashing the glass screen.

Back on *Oslo Queen 2*, Overn muttered an oath. '*Fa'en ta!* I missed him. Another split second and I'd have plugged them both. *Full fart*, skipper!'

In the motorboat, Kerr saw Ranby grab Yankovsky and raise a pistol to his head . . .

. . . *Rub, rub, r* . . . At last! His hands were free. He lurched unsteadily forwards towards the cockpit.

Before he could reach it, he was aware of the sound of a great rush of water — somewhere out in the fjord beyond the bows. A blinding orange-red light burst up from the sea and flooded the sky in an awesome golden hue. He stood and gazed as it steadily climbed towards the zenith with a terrible thundering noise. It took several seconds for the reality of the scene to smash its way through his mind's paralysis. Shock-waves smote his face. His ears cracked in pain. Fascinated, he watched a second missile rise from the sea, a third and then finally a fourth. The heavens were ablaze . . .

Aboard *Oslo Queen 2*, Cohen murmured, 'Holy mother of Moses! Armageddon — the Ragnarok . . . We're too late. We're too late . . .'

Oslo Queen 2's lights flooded the motorboat from stern to bow. She was almost alongside now. Overn took aim on the open sights of his rifle and fired at Ranby. It was point-blank range. Overn watched as the bullet entered the chest-cavity plumb dead centre. Ranby jerked and was already a corpse the instant he slumped to the deck. In the glare of the lights, Yankovsky turned to face them — his features grotesquely wild, his eyes stricken with abject terror. They saw Kerr move towards him. Yankovsky drew back and seemed to panic. Suddenly he was edging towards the starboard side. Kerr lunged out to grab him, tripped over Nilsen's corpse and crashed headlong — glancing his head on the bulwark. He lay still. Yankovsky looked down at Kerr, hesitated for a few seconds; then, with a terrible cry, leapt overboard and was immediately lost from view.

★ ★ ★

Six hours later the world's news agencies had their first reports hot on the wire:

BIG METEORITES QUESTION MARK FALL ACROSS NORTHERN EUROPE STOP MULTIPLE FIRE-BALLS LIGHT SKY FROM NORWAY TO MID-ATLANTIC STOP HUN-DREDS OF EYEWITNESSES REPORT UFOS STOP EVIDENCE CONFLICT-ING STOP ASTRONOMERS PUZZLED STOP

'They're not the only ones who are still puzzled,' remarked Cohen to Eriksen, shaking his head and tossing off the dregs of the only double brandy he'd ever drunk in his life. 'I still don't get it . . .'

The *Oslo Queen 2* had docked in Oslo several hours earlier. Everyone surviving the encounter in the fjord was now incommunicado — sealed off in a room in E-Gruppa's headquarters in Victoria Terrasse. There was a total media blackout. It was inquest time . . .

When Yankovsky had gone into the fjord, all but one man aboard *Oslo Queen 2* immediately forgot about him. Four Silent Men missiles were now apparently carrying their deadly nuclear warheads through the upper atmosphere towards Dimona in Israel. The fate of Yankovsky, the villain of the piece, was no longer of consequence.

From *Oslo Queen 2*, Cohen had immediately contacted his embassy in Oslo by radio telephone. Fortunately, being an E-Gruppa vessel, she operated a scrambler device so the rest of the world couldn't listen in to the somewhat hysterical conversation between him and his ambassador. The ambassador in turn had without delay alerted Tel Aviv — the message had come back that all personnel from Dimona had been evacuated . . .

The missiles never reached Dimona.

It was only later that Uri Cohen related how he remembered seeing the tall Russian colonel leap overboard from *Oslo Queen 2*. Neither Yankovsky nor the colonel had been seen again. At dawn the search in the fjord was joined by two helicopters but to no avail. Consensus among those who'd taken part in the fjord action was that Yankovsky in his panic to escape retribution had dragged down the colonel with him.

It was Kerr who inclined to the shade of opinion that Yankovsky, in his frenzy, had mistaken his tall countryman for Kovas. 'Poor sods,' said Kerr. 'We just let them drown. It was Yankovsky who did the right thing after all. He just retargeted those four Silent Men missiles and neutered their warheads with his box of tricks so they'd all fall harmlessly in mid-Atlantic . . . '

E-Gruppa, the PO and the CIA maintained their tight news blackout. At diplomatic level Russia, Israel and the UK readily co-operated. The CIA quickly 'arranged' for the Smithsonian Earth Watch Surveillance Group (generously funded via the CIA's own budget) to maintain the pretext of a major (multiple) meteorite fall in the northern hemisphere. Likewise, a Soviet astro-research group (motivated by the KGB) immediately lent support to the Americans' claim . . . And as if to compound the media's wide-spread confusion — as well as that of astronomers and space experts — some multiple hardware from the Soviet Cosmos-series launching had actually re-entered the atmosphere over southern Scandinavia and burned up spectacularly the very same night . . .

What evidence remained now lay in over 2,000 fathoms in the North Atlantic. Too deep and dangerous for even the know-how of the United States Navy to attempt to recover any part of it.

Disaster had been averted. For the sake of the fragile East-West détente, it was never going to be in the public's interest for any of those involved to reveal what had happened in the Oslo-fjord. The politicans — doves and hawks — either side breathed a consensus sigh of relief.

On the TWA flight back to Washington, Hines got out his portable and typed his prelim field-report. On arrival at Dulles, he handed it to Holmes. Holmes had already gassed transatlantic to Carpenter from the embassy in Oslo ... Without bothering to check his desk at Langley, Hines took off with Susie to West Palm Springs on his overdue two-week furlough. The Old Man, via Holmes, had grudgingly approved his immediate absence of leave. Anyway, the Department could play second fiddle for a change. It was Susie's turn. His marriage was more important to him than his career.

Meantime, at number 2 Dzerzhinsky Square, Major Tereshkova attended a KGB ceremonial eulogy spoken by General Kerbel for the late departed Colonel Zigel. Immediately after, she returned to her post in Oslo from where she promptly disappeared — taking with her several of Colonel Zigel's favourite possessions, including notes for a manuscript that she had secretly removed from his flat in Moscow.

In due course, E-Gruppa was able to close its files satisfactorily. One morning Oslo's *Aftenposten* carried a banner headline: LOCAL NEO-NAZI GROUP ARRESTED BY UNDERCOVER ACTION. ARMS CACHE FOUND . . .

Around the same time the *Aftenposten* carried another lesser news-item in eight-point type and placed in the announcement column known as *Ekteskap inngatt*.

It caught Overn's eye as he sat facing Presterud, his feet up on his desk, idly scanning the pages. 'Hey, chief! Happy endings! Listen to this: 'The marriage took place today between James Kerr of London, England, and Anna Solberg of Oslo'. Shouldn't we have sent flowers or something?'

The night Hines and his wife, Susie, returned to their Glendale duplex from West Palm Springs, the summons for a meeting with the big white chief — via Holmes's verbal instructions — was waiting there on his answerphone.

He dreaded that interview the following morning.

Around the table were the usual crowd — Doyle, Bentley, Willard and Holmes. Carpenter, as expected, chaired at the head of the table.

This time round, Hines knew he was the one with egg on his face. He could see Larry Holmes positively beaming at the prospect of being a ringside spectator to his subordinate's potential roasting by the Old Man.

'Shall we start, gentlemen,' said Carpenter with a neutral voice. 'As you all know by now, our recent exercise in Norway was . . . not quite as successful as we'd hoped it would be . . . '

Here it comes now, thought Hines, sitting at the far end of the table as remote from Carpenter as he'd been able to get. He was going to be publicly crucified on several counts in front of his betters. One count was going to be that compromising telephone call he'd made to Susie from Norway. Another was his big boob in Frogner Park with the KGB.

The Old Man had a reputation for indulging in the slow burn. Ignition now!

' . . . However,' began Carpenter again, with a benevolent twinkle in his eye. 'I think our junior colleague at the end of the table has to be congratulated on his . . . public relations foresight.'

Hines, confused, wondered what was going on. Maybe the Old Man had flipped his lid . . . Maybe the Old Man was just being sardonic! But Hines noted Holmes's eyes were puzzled too. This wasn't the scenario either had fantasised.

Carpenter, taking his time, picked up the green telephone nearest his right hand. 'Tell our visitors to step in now, Alice.' He replaced the receiver and then positively beamed down the table towards Hines; while he waited, Carpenter built a church to occupy his hands.

The door to the outer chamber opened. Hines first saw Alice, Carpenter's secretary, and then the very three people he'd never expected to see again. The tall one seemed instantly preoccupied by the portraits of past United States presidents hanging on the wall.

★ ★ ★

An hour later, standing in front of the Lincoln Memorial, the tall Russian, after a long silent spell, turned to Hines. 'Yes, it *was* worth coming to the West just to see it. Magnificent!'

'Then you've *all* decided to stay, Colonel Zigel?'

The colonel looked back at the Memorial, then he glanced quickly at Tanya and Yankovsky. When he turned to face Hines again, he answered, 'Do you also recall in Frogner Park we briefly discussed your poet Frost? . . . Correct me if I misquote him, but did he not once write: 'Home is the place where, when you have to go there, they *have* to take you in'.'

THE END

We do hope that you have enjoyed reading this large print book.

Did you know that all of our titles are available for purchase?

We publish a wide range of high quality large print books including:
Romances, Mysteries, Classics
General Fiction
Non Fiction and Westerns

Special interest titles available in large print are:
The Little Oxford Dictionary
Music Book, Song Book
Hymn Book, Service Book

Also available from us courtesy of Oxford University Press:
Young Readers' Dictionary
(large print edition)
Young Readers' Thesaurus
(large print edition)

For further information or a free brochure, please contact us at:
Ulverscroft Large Print Books Ltd.,
The Green, Bradgate Road, Anstey,
Leicester, LE7 7FU, England.
Tel: (00 44) **0116 236 4325**
Fax: (00 44) **0116 234 0205**

Other titles in the
Linford Mystery Library:

THAT INFERNAL TRIANGLE

Mark Ashton

An aeroplane goes down in the notorious Bermuda Triangle and on board is an Englishman recently heavily insured. The suspicious insurance company calls in Dan Felsen, former RAF pilot turned private investigator. Dan soon runs into trouble, which makes him suspect the infernal triangle is being used as a front for a much more sinister reason for the disappearance. His search for clues leads him to the Bahamas, the Caribbean and into a hurricane before he resolves the mystery.

THE GUILTY WITNESSES

John Newton Chance

Jonathan Blake had become involved in finding out just who had stolen a precious statuette. A gang of amateurs had so clever a plot that they had attracted the attention of a group of international spies, who habitually used amateurs as guide dogs to secret places of treasure and other things. Then, of course, the amateurs were disposed of. Jonathan Blake found himself being shot at because the guide dogs had lost their way . . .

THIS SIDE OF HELL

Robert Charles

Corporal David Canning buried his best friend below the burning African sand. Then he was alone, with a bullet-sprayed ambulance containing five seriously injured men and one hysterical nurse in his care. He faced heat, dust, thirst and hunger; and somewhere in the area roamed almost two hundred blood-crazed tribesmen led by a white mercenary with his own desperate reasons for catching up with the sole survivors of the massacre. But Canning vowed that he would win through to safety.

HEAVY IRON

Basil Copper

In this action-packed adventure, Mike Faraday, the laconic L.A. private investigator, stumbles by accident into one of his most bizarre and lethal cases when he is asked to collect a fifty thousand dollar debt by wealthy club owner, Manny Richter. Instead, Mike becomes involved in a murderous web of death, crime and corruption until the solution is revealed in the most unexpected manner.